'If I offered you the job and you accepted, there would be no room in your life for romance for some time to come. At the salary you're asking, I'd expect complete commitment,' said Matthew.

'I understand.' Thea felt as though she was selling her soul to the devil, and at some deeper level she realised that that might in fact be less dangerous than the pact this man was offering her. She didn't tell him that she'd had little time for romance anyway, not since the death of her parents and her inheritance of one trouble-mad teenage sister five years ago. 'I don't anticipate any problems on that score.' Her voice sounded a little bitter, even to her own ears.

A QUESTION OF TRUST

BY

SHIRLEY KEMP

MILLS & BOON LIMITED
ETON HOUSE   18-24 PARADISE ROAD
RICHMOND   SURREY   TW9 1SR

First published in Great Britain 1988
by Mills & Boon Limited

© Shirley Kemp 1988

Australian copyright 1988
Philippine copyright 1989
This edition 1989

ISBN 0 263 76232 7

Set in Plantin 11 on 11 pt.
05 – 8904 – 54918

Typeset in Great Britain by JCL Graphics, Bristol

Made and printed in Great Britain

CHAPTER ONE

'THEA!' Rita gasped, her face a study in disbelief. 'You don't mean you've actually applied for the job . . . not with Matthew Clayburn!'

Thea smiled, stifling the misgivings Rita's reaction resurrected. She squashed into a seat beside her friend and found a space on the table for her glass of bitter lemon. The pub was heaving with lunch-time drinkers.

'Not only applied,' she said, once she'd settled herself, 'but attended an interview this morning.'

Rita's mobile features openly displayed her disapproval.

'Well! You're a sly one! Why didn't you tell me before?'

Thea grimaced. 'Because I knew what you'd say, and I didn't want to be dissuaded. I need the money.'

'I know you're short of money, Thea . . . but . . . working for Matthew Clayburn . . .' She rolled her eyes to heaven. 'You're mad to even think of it.'

'You're right, of course,' Thea confirmed bitterly, 'but someone has to take care of Leon.'

Rita's lips thinned. 'Yes. Someone has to. So why don't you let his mother do it?'

Thea sighed. Rita was more irritated by her situation than she was herself. 'Melissa is Melissa,' she said. 'And no one can make her do anything she doesn't want to do.'

'That sister of yours is ruined . . . and she's never going to learn anything about responsibility as long

5

as you go on taking it for her.' Rita was reluctant to abandon her arguement. It was an old one, but, no matter how many times it was aired, it was never resolved.

'Melissa's got to be where the work is. She's a very good actress. All she needs is a chance,' Thea said, adding doggedly, 'It will be different when she's established herself. Meanwhile, there's still Leon.'

Rita shrugged, unconvinced, and Thea, who was far from convinced by her own explanations, changed the subject.

'Anyway, none of this matters, because I didn't get the job.'

'Didn't get it?' her friend repeated in astonishment. 'But you're the best secretary in the company. He can't have turned you down!'

'Not in so many words,' Thea smiled sardonically. 'But he will. Linda Prosser will see to it that he does.'

'Po-face Prosser! what's she got to do with it?'

Thea laughed. Rita's irreverance lightened her gloom.

'For some reason, she didn't seem to like me.'

'I can't imagine why,' Rita said ironically, as her eyes swept appraisingly over her friend's cream linen suit and violet blouse which so nearly matched her eyes, and up to her face with its flawless skin framed by thick, rich brown hair. 'You must have knocked Matthew Clayburn for six in that outfit. No wonder our Linda hated you. I hate you myself.'

Thea laughed. 'You're joking! This is the only decent suit I've got, and it's years old. Not a patch on what the elegant Miss Prosser was wearing, and she knew it. It made her very superior.' Thea's laughter subsided as she remembered the uncomfortable hour she'd just spent beneath the cool gaze of a pair of incredible cornflower-blue eyes. It was the first time she'd actually seen Matthew Clayburn, though she knew him well by reputation via the company grapevine, and she was unprepared for his startling good looks. For some reason, the shock undermined her confidence and she was sure she'd come across at the interview as stiff and awkward.

The interview had gone badly right from the start, and the personnel officer had done her best to compound the situation.

'Miss Prosser couldn't fault my credentials, as she was kind enough to tell Matthew Clayburn.' Thea unconsciously mimicked Linda Prosser's polite tones. 'But there was no way she could agree to my being given a higher salary scale than all the other top secretaries. So that was that.'

Thea bit her lip, recalling the humiliation she'd felt at Linda Prosser's implication of greed.

'We've set our own limit as to what a secretary's worth to the company, Miss Lawson,' she'd said, with emphasis on the 'we' to include Matthew Clayburn, and making it sound as though she ran the Trust with his assistance. 'But you obviously think you're worth a lot more.'

'Yes. I'm afraid I do.' Thea had met the strangely hostile grey eyes with a challenge.

Linda had smiled. 'Thank you for being so honest.' Her tone had conveyed satisfaction. She'd proffered the rope and watched Thea hang herself. 'Fortunately, there are other candidates, and hopefully they'll have a more realistic view of their value to the Trust.'

Thea had bitten back a tempting retort. Her gaze had shifted defiantly to the cornflower-blue eyes that had been watching her closely, and she'd addressed herself directly to Matthew Clayburn. 'If you've finished with me, I'd like to get back to the office. Tom Griffiths is waiting to give me dictation.'

She'd watched in fascination as a slow smile altered the sternly handsome face. The transformation took her by surprise, and she'd felt an unfamiliar fluttering sensation in the pit of her stomach. Holding her lips firmly together, she'd denied him an answering smile, and seen the slight lifting of his dark brow. He was a real charmer and no mistake, she'd admitted unwilling, and felt a mixture of regret and relief that she had so obviously burned her boats.

'Lucky Tom Griffiths,' he'd said at last, and Thea had seen the look of chagrined surprise on Linda Prosser's cool face.

He was flirting with her, Thea knew. Even in this situation he obviously had to live up to his reputation.

'We'll let you know, Miss Lawson,' Linda had said, her animosity hidden once more behind her careful mask.

'Don't call us—we'll call you.' Thea had spoken flippantly, unable to resist the opportunity to let them know she understood and didn't care.

'You're well out of it.' Rita's indignant voice brought Thea out of her reverie. 'You don't know what you'd have been letting yourself in for.'

'Oh, I think I do,' Thea replied wryly.

Everyone said that the job was a tough one and that Matthew Clayburn was virtually impossible to work for. Three first-class secretaries had bitten the dust in the past year, and word had got around that it would take a superwoman to handle the fiery Mr Clayburn with any degree of success.

'There were fifteen internal applicants,' she told

Rita. 'They obviously weren't put off by the grape-vine.'

'Like flies around the honeypot . . . ready to be squashed,' Rita said contemptuously. 'Personally, I don't know what women see in Matthew Clayburn.'

'Neither do I,' Thea said, and then added with a teasing grin, 'But he does have the most wonderful blue eyes.'

Rita's indignant splutter had them laughing all the way back to the Trust building. They parted at Thea's office door.

Tom Griffiths was already at his desk, his untidy head buried in a mass of paperwork. Thea felt a rush of affection and more than a tinge of relief. She hadn't really wanted to leave Tom for Matthew Clayburn, but the extra money had drawn her like a magnet. Even at the salary Linda Prosser had proposed, it would have meant a considerable increase. Perversely, Thea had pressed for more and lost.

'How did it go?' Tom looked up.

Thea shrugged. 'Not too well. I don't think you'll be getting rid of me quite yet.'

'Hmph!' Tom snorted disdainfully. 'I wouldn't have taken Clayburn for a fool. Still, his loss is my gain.' His smile was relieved. 'Now, perhaps we can get down to some work.'

Thea gave an exaggerated sigh and went to fetch her notebook.

But it wasn't the best afternoon's work she had ever done. Her mind kept wandering back to her interview and the chance she had thrown away. The thought of the extra money had driven her to apply, but, if she was honest, there had also been an element of challenge about the situation. Being denied the chance

to face up to that challenge was a bit of an anticlimax,
and it was that as much as anything else, she told
herself, that was the reason for her sense of depression.

It was a relief when five-thirty came. Thea washed
her hands in the small washbasin in Tom's room and
renewed her light make-up before taking the lift down
to the foyer. Matthew Clayburn was still in her mind,
and for a moment she thought she'd conjured him up
as the lift stopped and his broad figure entered. She
edged closer to the corner, hoping he hadn't noticed
her, taking cover behind an over-large woman from
accounts, but his eyes ruthlessly sought her out.

'Hello again, Miss Lawson.'

'Hello, Mr, Clayburn.'

Thea was flustered by the friendliness of his grin.
He had taken off his tie and the immaculate white
shirt she'd noticed earlier was opened at the throat,
revealing a strong column of tanned skin.

The lift bounced to a halt and Thea moved forward,
hoping to get quickly past him, but he blocked her
way.

'Rushing to keep a date, Miss Lawson?'

'As a matter of fact. I am.' Thea was conscious of
the curious sidelong glances of the large woman, and
as the doors parted she darted out into the foyer.

'Goodbye, Mr Clayburn,' she called, half turning
her head to look behind. She was startled to feel a
touch on her arm and to hear his deep laugh close to
her ear.

'I'm right here beside you.'

'So I see.'

Thea was annoyed to feel the colour flooding her
cheeks and flashed an irritated glance at his smiling
face. What did he want? she asked herself furiously.

To gloat over the mess she'd made of the interview? Hardly. Whatever else he was, she didn't think Matthew Clayburn was petty.

Grimly, she pushed at the large exit door and hurried out into the evening sunshine, dismayed to find he was still beside her.

She turned, hoping to leave him there, but he put out a large hand and grasped her elbow. Despite the firmness of his hold, there was no discomfort in it and Thea was struck by the gentleness he unconsciously exhibited.

'I wish to speak with you, Miss Lawson.'

There was nothing gentle about his words. They had a steely edge that brought her eyes up to his face. She stared at him uncertainly, wishing she had the nerve to ask him outright what he wanted. He'd been flirting with her earlier, disarming her with those wonderful eyes. Had she been quick enough to guard her response, or had he seen through to the flare of excitement he'd engendered? Was he lining her up as a candidate for one of his famous 'affairs'? Not if she had anything to do with it, she vowed silently.

'I'm sorry, but I'm in rather a hurry,' she said firmly. 'Can't it wait until tomorrow morning?'

'I'm afraid not. This isn't a request—it's an order.'

Thea felt outraged. He was using his position as managing director to browbeat her.

'But it's not convenient,' she said defiantly. Thursday was the one night a week Aunt Edith allowed herself to have off to eat out with a friend, and the one night Thea had Leon all to herself. She'd promised to be home by seven, and the latest possible train would leave in less then half an hour.

Caught in Matthew Clayburn's determined gaze, Thea grew angry. 'The Trust pays me only until five-thirty, Mr Clayburn. Outside of that time, your orders don't count.'

Dark brows drew together over suddenly steely eyes. 'Money seems to matter an awful lot to you, Miss Lawson. Quite frankly, it surprises me.'

Thea felt the tightening of her stomach muscles. It was the second time today that she'd been subtly accused of being grasping, and this time she had nothing to lose by defending herself.

'Perhaps it would mean as much to you if you didn't have it,' she said harshly. She was tempted to ask him what he knew of juggling with pennies each month, stretching them so thinly they became threadbare . . . and then, at the end of it all, having to take money from an old woman whose savings were already dwindling fast. She bit her lip to keep herself from flinging a few home truths at him, but her eyes were unable to hide her fury.

A gleam of amusement softened his gaze. 'And besides, it's not my business,' he said. 'Is that what you wanted to say, Miss Lawson?'

Thea flushed. 'Something like that.' He was still holding her elbow and she pulled it free. 'Now if you don't mind, I've a train to catch.'

'If you would kindly reconsider, and spare me a few moments of your very valuable time, you might find it worth your while,' he said with a mocking smile. 'And I'd be prepared to drive you home afterwards. You might even knock minutes off your obviously tight schedule.'

Thea shook her head, flustered by his persistence. 'Is there a point to all this, Mr Clayburn?'

'Of course. I should have thought that was obvious.' The slow, transforming smile that had set her heart pounding at the interview had the same effect now.

She held her breath and waited. Was he actually going to proposition her here and now . . . in so many words? 'Does your reluctance mean you've changed your mind about wanting the job?'

Thea swallowed her breath, taken completely by surprise. 'Do . . . do . . . you mean . . .? But I thought . . .' Her heart began to pound. 'Are you . . . offering me the job?' She coloured hotly, embarrassed by her earlier interpretation of his intentions.

'Not quite,' he said sardonically. 'But I thought we might talk about it. There are a number of points we didn't cover this morning.'

Bemused, Thea continued to stare at him, and he laughed.

'Do I take it you agree to talk to me, Miss Lawson?'

'Yes . . . I'm sorry . . . I mean . . . yes . . .'

'Good. Then let's find somewhere a little less public.'

Thea allowed him to lead her against the flow of the rushing commuters. They walked in silence, his hand tucked into her arm, its pressure filling her with a strange mixture of exhilaration and apprehension.

She looked up at him; he seemed tall and withdrawn now as he engrossed himself in the business of reaching his destination, and she felt a tremor of doubt. Was she up to dealing with this man? Rita had been right. There would be no comfortable level on which to conduct a relationship with him, in business or otherwise. His dominant personality made him a man to be loved or hated—with no half measures. Thea wondered if his last three secretaries had loved him before they hated him.

'Where are we going?' she asked at last.

'There's a small coffee-shop around the next corner. Will that suit you?'

'Yes.' Thea nodded, made breathless from the fast walk his long legs impelled. 'But I have to make a phone call.'

Aunt Edith would understand. She didn't say, of course, but Thea knew she was beginning to worry about her dwindling finances. Thea had been reluctant to tell her aunt about her interview in case she had to disappoint her. Now . . . if there was a chance of getting the job, after all . . . she might not have to.

Matthew Clayburn swung her deftly through the doorway of a small coffee-shop and indicated a cowled booth in one corner. 'The phone's over there.'

Thea weaved a path through the closely set tables, noting that he sat in the far corner with a grimly impatient look on his face. She made her explanatory phone call short and crossed to him quickly.

As she seated herself opposite to him, he looked at her with a cynical curl of his lips. 'It's better to keep a lover waiting than a boss.'

Thea's eyes flashed anger at this obvious and unnecessary baiting. 'I was only a few moments, and he . . .'

She cut the rest of her sentence short. She'd been about to say that Leon wasn't her lover but her nephew, but remembered in time one of the stipulations he'd put to her that morning and stopped herself.

'You were about to say?' Matthew Clayburn's dark brows lifted expectantly.

'Nothing. It's not important.' She shrugged. 'Do you think we could come to the point?'

He studied her face, which she knew was hot from rushing and from her swallowed-back anger. She set her lips tightly, suffering his scrutiny, and waited.

'The question I asked this morning about personal ties wasn't frivolous, Miss Lawson.'

'I didn't think it was.' Thea felt uncomfortable and a little guilty. She hadn't exactly lied when she answered that question, but it hadn't seemed the moment to mention a year-old baby.

'If I offered you the job and you accepted, there would be no room in your life for romance for some time to come. At the salary you're asking, I'd expect complete commitment.'

'I understand.' Thea felt as though she was selling her soul to the devil, and at some deeper level she realised that that might in fact be less dangerous than the pact this man was offering her. She didn't tell him that she'd had little time for romance anyway, not since the death of her parents and her inheritance of one trouble-mad teenage sister five years ago. 'I don't anticipate any problem on that score.' Her voice sounded a little bitter, even to her own ears.

The dark brows rose again. 'And tonight's date?'

She shifted uncomfortably. 'Nothing important.'

'Forgive me—but that's not the impression I received. You seemed pretty anxious to be on time.' He smiled. 'Always a mistake, I might add . . . to be too eager.'

'I'm sure you'd know much more about that than me, Mr Clayburn,' Thea fumed. 'But your advice, in this instance, is inappropriate.'

He went on looking at her for a few seconds longer and then nodded.

'OK,' he said crisply. 'So let's get down to business I need a secretary right away . . . one who's able to take off with me at the drop of a hat.'

Thea was jolted into attention. Had the question of travel come up at the interview this morning? If it had, she hadn't caught the implication. Perhaps she'd been drowning in cornflower-blue seas at the time. She was careful not to do so now as he turned his gaze intently on her.

'There are a number of impending deals abroad and I need to have my secretary along to take verbatim notes and to act as a witness to any agreements that take place. Any problems so far?'

Thea shook her head as calmly as she could. Inside, her brain was buzzing with anxiety. Was it really practicable for her to take this job? Could she really expect Aunt Edith to cope with that kind of situation almost single-handedly? 'I shouldn't think so.'

'You don't sound too positive, Miss Lawson.' Matthew Clayburn frowned. 'Remember what I said about commitment.'

'I remember, Mr Clayburn.' She couldn't hide her irritation. 'But you haven't offered me the job yet, so I don't see any point in being too positive.'

His deep chuckle was a surprise and almost disarmed Thea.

'Taking a secretary, like a new love, is always a lottery, Miss Lawson,' he said, his eyes raking her in a sudden outrageous challenge. 'But I'm willing to take a chance, if you are.'

If she hadn't needed the money she might have smacked his mocking face. Instead, she held out her hand.

'If the job carries my asking price,' she said, 'I accept your offer.'

He grinned, and his big hand enveloped hers. 'Done!' he said.

Aunt Edith was in the kitchen, spooning creamed potato into Leon's open mouth. Thea kissed her cheek and slumped down at the table.

'How's he been?'

'Fine.' The older woman's face broke into a warm smile. 'He's no trouble at all—bless him.'

Thea's fingers touched the little boy's silky curls. 'I wish we could say the same for his mother,' she said with a sigh. 'Did we get a letter today?'

Edith Lawson shook her head. 'You know Melissa better than that, dear.'

Thea felt suddenly tired, and a vague feeling of depression took hold of her.

'It wouldn't hurt Melissa to drop us a line now and again, to let us know where she is and when she might be coming home.' She made a small, furious sound. 'Doesn't she ever worry about her son?'

Edith had finished feeding Leon and was wiping his face with a warm, damp cloth.

'He's safe and well looked after here,' she said complacently. 'I'm only grateful that Melissa didn't suggest taking him with her. Just imagine! Dragging the poor little mite around all those draughty theatres . . . sleeping goodness knows where . . .'

Thea took the baby from her aunt and hugged him. He was so sweet and trusting. He smiled up at her with clear blue eyes and Thea smoothed his thick, silky hair, darker at birth, but already growing lighter. At first, he'd looked like Melissa, but he was changing.

'I wish Melissa had told us more about his father,' she said, frowning in frustration. 'At least to tell us his name. I feel we're entitled to know.'

'Melissa doesn't think so.' Edith Lawson reclaimed Leon and hugged him to her. 'And I can't help feeling grateful to him . . . whoever he is.'

Thea gave her a worried frown. 'Edith—don't get

too wrapped up in Leon. One of these days Melissa will come back for him . . . and then you'll get hurt.'

Her aunt nodded. 'I know . . . And that's as it should be. But I'm happy for now and I'm going to make the most of it.' She sighed. 'My brother and your mother were all the family I had . . . and you and Melissa, of course. Leon is a gift . . . a loaned one maybe . . .'

Thea couldn't bear the expression on her aunt's face and got up to fill the kettle, hiding the anxiety which gnawed at her.

With Leon in bed. the two women chatted comfortably over dinner. Thea told Edith her news.

'I got the job with Matthew Clayburn.' Her voice was tinged with anxiety, and Edith picked it up at once.

'Are you sure you want it?'

'Yes. I mean . . . yes, but I've been told I'll have to travel and I'm worried about you and Leon. I know you say you're happy . . . but even so you'll be tied more than ever . . . and it doesn't seem fair.'

Thea's anguish held more than a hint of anger—at Matthew Clayburn for his determined self-interest; at Melissa for her selfish disregard of her own son; and at herself for her secret desire for her own freedom. But she couldn't take it at her aunt's expense.

'Oh, damn!' Thea cursed. 'It isn't going to be possible, is it? I mean . . . we'll have more money, but that's not the prime consideration, is it?'

Edith reached for Thea's hand. 'No, it isn't. The prime consideration is you. And it's more than time you had something for yourself. I've just told you I'm perfectly happy with things the way they are for now, so the only question is . . . do you want this job?'

Thea met her aunt's gaze doubtfully. But despite

her misgivings a feeling of exhilaration was beginning inside.

'Yes, I think I do.'

'Then take it, my dear. And be happy.'

She arrived in the office the following morning to find a disgruntled Tom scowling into the first cup of coffee of the day. His scowl included her as he looked up and said without preamble, 'I thought you told me yesterday that you didn't get the job.'

Thea groaned. The grapevine had obviously been working through the night! She'd been hoping to get in early to tell Tom herself and soften the blow, but it was twenty to nine before she'd arrived.

'I didn't think I had. Matthew Clayburn caught me on the way home and sprang the offer on me.' She sighed and sat down opposite. 'How did you find out?'

Tom grunted. 'Miss Prosser was at my door fifteen minutes ago. Apparently her great white chief had despatched her to find you. He wants to see you in his office.' He cocked a teasing eyebrow at her. 'She didn't seem any more pleased than I am about your new appointment.'

'I can imagine.' Thea bit her lip. 'Oh Tom, I'm sorry. But I won't leave you in the lurch, I promise. I'll give you a month's notice and help you find a suitable replacement.'

'You're in no position to give any such promises. Miss Lawson.'

The deep voice brought a startled Thea around to face the stony-faced man standing in the doorway. He was wearing a steel-grey suit that exactly matched the cold gleam in his eyes. He crossed the room to tower over her as she sat almost mesmerised by the power of his presence.

'Linda said you hadn't yet arrived. When you start work for me on Monday morning. I'll expect you to leave such bad habits as unpunctuality behind.'

'Monday morning!' Thea ignored the gibe about her uncharacteristic lateness, looking at him incredulously. 'But I can't start work for you on Monday. What about Tom?'

A glimmer of amusement shone in the blue eyes. 'Your anxiety is unnecessary. I've asked Linda Prosser to fix Tom up with the best typist in the pool.'

Thea burned with indignation. The suggestion that any typist from the pool could simply step in and take over her job cut her to the quick.

'That's a very high-handed action, Mr Clayburn,' she said hotly. 'Especially since Tom hasn't agreed yet to releasing me.'

He was still for a moment, studying her face with an inscrutable expression. He seemed to be weighing something up in his mind. An uncomfortable, breathless sensation caught Thea unawares. Had he changed his mind about giving her the job? She was surprised at how much the thought upset her, and half wished she hadn't lost her temper.

When finally he spoke, his voice was hard with anger. 'Let's get one thing straight. I've no time to go pussy-footing around making sure I don't tread on anyone's corns. This is a business, not a charm school. We're none of us here to learn the social graces or to cultivate sensitivities.' He fixed her with a harsh stare. 'I need an assistant . . . now . . . full stop.'

He paused to let his words sink in, and Thea found she couldn't meet his eyes.

After a while, he went on, 'Since you applied for the job, I assume you want it, which means leaving Tom Griffiths at some point. Now, it doesn't seem to me to matter much when that happens from Tom's point of view, but from my point of view, the move is very important . . . . I might say crucial . . . so my needs come first.'

And his needs always would come first, Thea was sure. She chewed at her lip, intimidated by his fury, but still rebellious. She turned from him to look at Tom, who was sitting quietly, his eyes moving from one to the other.

'Look at me when I'm speaking to you.'

Thea heard his hiss of fury and her eyes flew up to meet his blazing blue gaze. She flinched as his hand came out to grasp her arm and haul her to her feet, drawing her to him so that his tight, angry face was uncomfortably close.

'If your skin is thin, you won't do for this job. Yesterday, I thought you showed spirit and common sense. Maybe I made a mistake.'

Her own anger kindled in response to his. 'I'm aware that you're trying to put me in the wrong,' she cried, her eyes spitting fire at him. 'But I see nothing thin-skinned about expecting a little common courtesy. I'm thinking more of Tom than my-self.'

'A commendable display of loyalty, Miss Lawson.' His smile was unpleasant. 'I hope I inspire as much.'

Thea blinked, shaken and unsure of herself.

'Then . . . you mean . . you still want me?'

The hard look remained in his eyes, but he released his hold on her arm. She stood back from him, absently rubbing at her smarting skin, a feeling of

weakness in her limbs and a sense of self-disgust at her
obvious relief.

'I think I can say yes to that.'

His blue eyes mocked her . . . challenged her . . .
fired her with heat.

Thea gasped, aware of a mounting tension. Words
of defiance formed in her throat, but remained
unuttered.

Matthew Clayburn waited for her response and,
receiving none, he smiled with obvious satisfaction.
'I'll expect to see you on Monday. Don't be late.'

He turned to leave and then stood in the doorway to
look back.

Thea stared at him, bemused by the strength of her
own conflicting emotions. The rapidity of her
breathing proclaimed the heady excitement she felt,
even as her mind denied it. The memory of his hand
holding her fiercely remained, to thrill, even though
the burning cruelty of his hold outraged her.

'By the way,' he said casually. 'I hope I made myself
clear yesterday. This job will take up all of your
energies. There'll be no time for outside
commitments. No ties of any kind.' His lip curled
cynically. 'The man you were rushing to meet last
night . . .' He paused, fixing her with a narrow blue
stare. 'I hope he understands the situation.'

Thea, indignant, opened her mouth to tell him that
her 'date' had been her sister's child, but caught
herself up in time. Would he consider Leon a
'commitment', an unacceptable tie? And, as to
emotional attachment, she found herself reluctant to
acknowledge the barren nature of her social life. In
the past five years there'd been precious little time to
form attachments. All of her attention and energy
seemed to have been taken up with Melissa's

problems of one kind or another, but that wasn't Matthew Clayburn's business.

'He understands perfectly,' she said, after some thought, and added with a flash of devilment, 'He doesn't seem to mind being patient. Perhaps he thinks I'm worth waiting for.'

She felt a small stab of satisfaction as his face turned grim, but a faint chill crept up her spine as he fixed her with his icy gaze.

'I'm sure he does,' he said, softly sibilant. 'But you won't find me as patient, Miss Lawson.' He gave her an intense, enigmatic look and then added, 'I'll expect you in my office at eight-thirty sharp on Monday.'

'Phew!' Tom let out his breath as Matthew Clayburn left his office. His eyes rolled upwards. 'I hope you know what you're letting yourself in for, my girl.'

Thea sat down heavily. Her legs were weak and her heart was still beating too rapidly for comfort.

'I hope I do, too.' She heaved a long-drawn-out sigh. 'If it wasn't for the money . . .' But the money was suddenly irrelevant. She knew that if the job had come with a reduction in salary, she would still have taken it. He'd thrown her a challenge and she fully intended to take him up on it. She felt a resolute stiffening of her spine and she smiled into Tom's still doubtful face.

'Don't worry, Tom. I intend to give him a good run for his money.'

Tom snorted sourly. 'It's time someone did.' He reached across his desk to pat her hand. 'Just make sure you run fast enough to stay out of trouble.'

Tom's words conjured up a startling picture of herself running, with Matthew Clayburn in hot pursuit. It was even more startling to find she was already wondering what would happen if she stopped suddenly and let him catch her. She shrugged the dangerous images away, but his handsome face remained in her mind's eye.

Instinct warned her that the pleasing features were a distraction from the real core of the man. Beneath was a ruthless ego, and the foundation upon which he had built his successful career.

'I think I'll manage,' she said to Tom, but heard the doubt in her own voice.

Later, over dinner, Edith wanted to know more about Matthew Clayburn. 'What kind of a man is your new boss?'

Thea hesitated. The question was a tricky one, because she had yet to make up her mind as to what kind of man he was. The antagonism he kindled in her bordered on dislike, but she had to admit there was a subtle fascination about the way he admitted no obstacles in the path of what he wanted.

And she had a shrewd suspicion that, despite the extra money, Edith might not be so approving if she realised that Thea was swapping a nice, easy-going man like Tom Griffiths for an unknown quantity like Matthew Clayburn, whose reputation was against him.

'Quite a handsome man,' she said guardedly, and then laughed at the look that was dawning in her aunt's eyes. 'Oh, no! Not my type, I'm afraid. And I'm sure I'm not his.'

Edith snorted indignantly. 'If you're not, then he can't be a very discerning man.'

Thea laughed and squeezed Edith's hand gratefully. 'Not everyone views me through your rose-coloured spectacles.'

'Nonsense! You always were a beautiful child, and now you're a beautiful woman with a lovely nature.' Edith sighed. 'It's high time you found a man to appreciate those qualities.'

Thea found herself flushing. 'The last thing I want in my life right now is a man. It would only complicate matters.' She grinned sourly. 'My new boss expressly stipulated no romantic ties.'

Edith's smile was sly. 'Interesting. Perhaps he has plans in that direction himself.'

Thea laughed the ridiculous idea away. 'Rubbish!' All the man wants is a secretary . . . and that's what he'll get.'

She pushed down a strange surge of anticipation and determined to clarify her thinking with regard to her prospective new boss. She was to be Matthew Clayburn's personal assistant, and it would need all her powers of concentration to meet what she knew would be very exacting demands. If she was going to confuse the issue by allowing herself to become involved on any other level, then she was going to make things unnecessarily difficult.

Nevertheless, over the weekend, she found herself going carefully through her sparse wardrobe, planning ways to mix and match and expand, and hoping Matthew Clayburn wouldn't notice how limited was her choice. With her first month's salary cheque, she vowed, she would have to spend money on some new clothes.

CHAPTER TWO

RITA was crossing the foyer of the Trust building as Thea rushed in on Monday morning. She gave Thea a frowning look.

'You might have told me. I was practically the last to know.'

Thea groaned. 'Don't start a quarrel now, Rita. I'm late. I'll see you later . . . for coffee . . .'

'I might not be free,' Rita said stubbornly.

'Come to think of it, I might not be either.'

Thea rushed past her friend, knowing without glancing back that a look of outrage followed her progress across to the lifts, but she had no time to worry about anyone's hurt feelings at the moment.

She'd slept restlessly and woken with a start. By the time she'd sorted out what she was going to wear from her meagre wardrobe and changed a pair of shoes with an inexplicably loose heel for the deep lilac ones she'd worn to her interview, she'd made herself late. Out of breath and wound up with tension, she was too impatient to wait for the lift and took three flights of stairs at a run.

It was just three minutes off eight-thirty, and she had no intention of letting Matthew Clayburn tell her again that he wouldn't tolerate unpunctuality.

She was panting with exertion by the time she'd arrived outside the door of his office suite, and she stood for some seconds, allowing herself the time to regain her composure, before taking a deep breath and entering.

The room in which her interview had taken place was the boardroom and quite imposing, but it was nothing in comparison to the almost opulent suite she now entered.

The outer office was empty and, moving tentatively to the inner office, Thea was surprised to find that empty, too. Relief mixed with anticlimax. Having worked herself up all weekend for that first confrontation, she felt let down. She had half expected to see him sitting behind his desk, stop-watch in hand, to see if she dared to be late.

However, his absence did give her the chance to look around, to get to know the layout a little before he put in an appearance. The place was beautifully furnished, pin neat, and had all the latest office equipment, including a word processor with a large, freestanding printer as well as an electronic typewriter. Thea guessed that Matthew Clayburn would be a stickler for having a job done properly.

It was a surprise, therefore, to find the filing system was in chaos. The shiny new cabinets were unlocked and opened to reveal a clutter of files overflowering with papers which, after a brief perusal, Thea found to be haphazard and out of date order. The question was, did he like them this way or was the chaos one of the reasons why his last secretary had left in a hurry?

Recalling her interview and the way he'd spelled out his expectations of her, she decided that the latter was the case and heaved a sigh. Oh, well! Nothing for it but to plunge in at the deep end, she told herself philosophically. And anyway, there was nothing like a journey through a filing system for putting one in the picture. It looked like being a long job, but would undoubtedly be worth the effort in knowledge gained.

She was kneeling on the floor with files and papers

spread around on the carpet, deeply engrossed in her self-appointed task, when she suddenly became aware of a pair of black, highly polished shoes. They were standing in a small, circular space between the paperwork, and contained a pair of feet attached to long legs encased in dark blue suiting. It took a moment or two for her to detach her attention from the files and to follow the legs upwards to the tall figure which towered above her.

He had an amused, faintly disbelieving expression on his face, and his eyes dazzled her anew with their depth of blue.

'My dear Miss Lawson! What on earth are you doing?'

Thea flushed and scrambled hastily to her feet.

'I'm trying to sort out this . . . mess.' Her arms swept an arc above the jumble of papers littering the carpet. 'It isn't easy.'

His mouth twisted cynically. 'I'm sure it isn't.'

He looked terrific this morning, Thea had grudgingly to admit. His dark blue suit had a faint stripe of grey, and he wore a pearl grey shirt with a grey and navy tie. His dark hair was carefully brushed and shone with cleanliness, and Thea caught the faint scent of his tangy aftershave. A real lady-killer, she thought disparagingly, but couldn't deny the quickening of her pulse, and wondered if he had disturbed his other secretaries as much. Very likely, she thought grimly, and it was probably the reason why the filing system was in chaos. It would be very difficult to concentrate with Matthew Clayburn around, unless one was very determined. She took an instant vow that she would be very, very determined, and stay well outside the aura of his magnetic pull.

And, seeing the derisory light in his eyes as he surveyed the mess of papers on the floor, she was sure he would have no qualms about getting rid of any woman, secretary or lover, if she did not measure up to his high expectations.

'Just dump that lot back where you got them from for now. I want to talk to you.'

Thea gave a small cry of dismay. She had just begun to create some order among the first few files. To 'dump' them as he had ordered would mean that she would have to start again from scratch.

'Can't you give me half an hour to put them away carefully?' she protested. 'It seems such a waste of time to mix them up again.'

His hard eyes swept her up and down impatiently. 'Don't waste *my* time in arguing. Just do as I say.'

He swept on through into his office, scattering papers as he went.

With fumbling fingers that shook, partly from nerves and partly fury, Thea gathered up the files and papers and thrust them back into the cabinet, sliding the drawer shut with a defiant slam.

'Come in when you're ready.' The cool voice called from the other office and, seething inwardly, Thea gritted her teeth and went into his room.

He was pulling a mass of paperwork from his briefcase and arranging it carefully on his desk as she sat down opposite to him. It was some time before he looked up, and Thea thought furiously that it was all right for *him* to waste *her* time.

He glanced up at last and an impatient frown flitted across his face. 'You'll need a notebook and pencil. That is, unless you have an exceptional memory.'

Thea bit her lip at the sarcasm and jumped to her feet, seething as she rummaged in her newly acquired desk for a notebook and pencil, vowing that in future, she would give him as few chances as possible to catch her out.

'That's better,' he said, as she sat down once more in the chair opposite. 'Now, perhaps we can make a start.'

Thea kept her eyes lowered so that he couldn't see the murderous impulse that gleamed there.

For the next hour, she took notes on every aspect of her job, with the names and relevant departments of all personnel she was likely to encounter on his behalf, as well as the names of clients with whom he was currently involved. His briefing was comprehensive and, she had to admit, would be very useful to her.

'You can type that lot up or transfer it to a special book for your own information, whichever you decide,' he said at last. 'Later on, I'll get someone to take you around the relevant departments and introduce you as my assistant. You might already know some of the people involved, but it won't do any harm to make personal contact, so that they recognise you as being attached to me.'

Thea's heart gave a bump. Attached to him! Yes, she thought wryly . . . just as an arm is attached to a torso . . . as a slave is attached to its master. Already he was taking her for granted, and no doubt she would very soon become near invisible, except as a means of translating his demands into reality. She smiled grimly to herself.

'Have I said something amusing?'

His cold voice made her start guiltily, as she realised she'd been staring into space, engrossed in her cynical thoughts for some minutes. She pulled herself hastily together.

'No, Mr Clayburn,' she said demurely, gaining

some satisfaction from his frown of annoyance.

'I've called a meeting for ten-thirty this morning of all the managers involved in the new scheme I'm setting up,' he said sharply. 'I'd like you to take notes. It will put you in the picture as to what it's all about.'

Thea's heart sank. It was some time since she'd taken minutes at a meeting, and her shorthand was a little rusty. 'Am I to take them verbatim?'

He gave her a cynical smile. 'Could you?'

She frowned back at him. 'Probably. But I couldn't guarantee it.'

His smile widened until it was almost friendly. 'Then I'll let you off the hook for today, since you're new in the department.'

'Thanks for nothing,' she muttered beneath her breath, but she was glad of the concession, and vowed to brush up on her shorthand. She was beginning to know him better and thought he would play on any weakness she might be foolish enough to display.

'Just listen carefully and watch me,' he broke into her thoughts. 'I'll give you the nod when I want you to take notes.'

It was a hectic morning. Thea was just typing up the notes he'd given her when the first of the visitors arrived.

He was a broad-shouldered blond with warm brown eyes, which lit up as she lifted her head to enquire his business.

'So, you're the new secretary, eh?' His voice was boyish and friendly. 'Matthew certainly knows how to pick them.'

She wasn't offended by his teasing, and as he held out a large hand to her she put her own into it and felt instinctively that he was a man she could trust. His candid gaze was admiring, but held no hint of a leer.

'I bet you say that to all his secretaries,' she quipped, and his laugh echoed around the office.

'I don't. But I see what you mean. He has had rather a lot of them, hasn't he?' He studied her with a roguish twinkle. 'But I'm willing to bet that you'll stay the course.'

'Thea is a secretary, Mike, not a filly.' The cool voice startled them both and Thea flushed scarlet, partly from surprise at hearing her first name on his lips and partly from anxiety. Had he heard her part in the discussion? It was hard to say as his cool look brushed her face.

'Besides, it's too early to place bets. You might get better odds later on.'

He crossed the room to shake the man by the hand. 'Glad you got here early,' he said more cordially. 'There are one or two points I'd like to iron out with you before the meeting starts.' He indicated Thea, who was watching the interchange. 'I might as well introduce you formally to my new assistant, Thea Lawson. This is Mike Donovan, who will be overall manager of the new loans scheme.'

Mike gave Thea a wink. 'Nice to meet you. I'm sure we'll be seeing a lot of each other.'

Matthew Clayburn gripped his elbow. 'Not as much as you'd like. Thea is going to be very busy.' He began to propel Mike towards his office. 'And so are you. I don't want any slip-ups on this business.'

He took Mike into his office and closed the door behind them, leaving Thea with a feeling of having been deliberately shut out. The last look he had given her over his shoulder had told her quite clearly that he disapproved of her fraternising with his underlings.

Well, let him disapprove, she thought rebelliously,

and made a rude grimace at his retreating back before turning once more to her notes.

In the event, she had little time to dwell on her feelings. The other members of the meeting began arriving thick and fast, and Thea had her work cut out to deal with them all. The small cloakroom was soon cluttered with coats and hats, and her office was bursting at the seams with men.

In answer to her slightly harassed announcement over the intercom of the arrival of his visitors, Matthew Clayburn barked an order for her to settle them into the small boardroom to the rear of the suite. There were twenty in all, and it was a bit of a squeeze, but at last, amid much good-humoured banter, she managed to get them all settled just as Matthew entered with Mike Donovan in tow.

Somehow, Thea had managed to photocopy the paperwork and ensure that in front of every man was a neat file of relevant papers, a notepad and a pen, and she acknowledged the sardonic nod of approval Matthew Clayburn gave her with a tight smile Her face felt hot and she hoped fervently that she didn't look as flustered as she felt.

He further disconcerted her, however, by taking her arm and calling the meeting to order to introduce her, and she was glad when he indicated she should take her seat beside him. It was at this point she realised that the only person without a notepad and pencil was herself.

He nodded coldly to her whispered explanation and indicated she should go and get it. His frown of disapproval as she returned further disconcerted her. However, once she'd become engrossed in the meeting, she forgot her nerves and became interested, listening carefully to the opinions and ideas expressed and making abbreviated notes in answer to Matthew Clayburn's curt nods.

Once or twice, his hand touched hers lightly to indicate she should stop writing and simply listen, and each time it happened she felt an electric current flow up her arm and prayed that the heat in her cheeks wasn't visible. And once or twice she caught Mike Donovan's eye, giving him a furtive smile in answer to his wink of encouragement.

About half-way throught the meeting, Matthew lowered his dark head to hers and whispered that she should see about some coffee. His breath was warm against her cheek and she could smell the subtle freshness of his aftershave. She was taken by surprise at the curling movement of her toes and the slight feeling of breathlessness she experienced as his shoulder brushed hers.

She knocked her knee against the table as she stood up and didn't dare to look at him as she fled the room, afraid to see the look of contempt she knew would be there in his face. What was it about him that made her feel such a clumsy and inept fool?

In the small but well-equipped kitchen, she leaned against the unit and took a deep steadying breath, calling up the reserves of her self-confidence. The cool, professional calm she'd always taken for granted seemed to have deserted her, swept away by a pair of critical blue eyes.

Pull yourself together, she told herself sternly. Even Matthew Clayburn couldn't expect a flawless performance on her first day.

She wished she'd thought ahead to the probability of a coffee-break, but thought he might have mentioned it beforehand and given her time to get acquainted with the facilities of the kitchen. She did a quick round, opening and shutting doors, sighing with relief as one opened to reveal neatly stacked crockery. There was a large coffee percolator on the work surface and coffee grounds in the cupboard over the sink, but no instant. She realised, with a sense of panic, that it was going to take ages to get the percolator going.

There was a strange. cold sensation in the back of her neck, and Thea was almost tearful with frustration. Had he done this on purpose to test her mettle? Well, she'd show him some of that after the meeting broke up.

The touch of a hand on her shoulder was close to the last straw, and with a strangled cry she swung around to stare into Matthew Clayburn's mocking face, swaying a little with the shock.

'Take it easy,' he said, and his tone was almost kind. He took hold of her by the waist and steadied her against him. 'I didn't think you were the sort to get yourself in a state. Calm down.'

Even those words of intended comfort had an accusatory ring and Thea went cold with fury. She jerked herself free of his hold and took a deep shuddering breath.

'Oh, didn't you? And I suppose that in your super-efficient way you didn't think it necessary to warn me about the coffee. I could have had the percolator going earlier, before the meeting began. Or was I supposed to use my psychic intuition to work that one out for myself?'

'I said calm down.'

With infuriating coolness, he pulled her to him again, casually holding her to him with one arm. With his free hand, he lifted the receiver of the wall telephone, punching the buttons with a firm finger.

Thea, feeling the uncomfortable effect of his hard body against hers, longed to wriggle out of his grasp, but feared she would appear even more of a fool if he refused to let her go.

'Maria,' he said into the handset, 'we're ready for coffee now.'

He replaced the receiver and turned to her, placing his free hand on her shoulder.

She stiffened and opened her mouth, not quite knowing what she was going to say but angrily determined to say it, but he put his finger to her lips.

'Hush, my dear Miss Lawson,' he said, with an indulgent note in his voice. 'Whatever you were going to say, you're probably quite right. I did forget to tell you about the coffee, which is why I came out now, to repair the omission. You see? I can admit I'm not perfect. Normally, we will use the percolator, of course, but for today I thought it best for the kitchen staff to deal with the coffee-break.'

She gasped as she saw his eyes narrow and fix on her lips. For one incredible moment, she felt the feather-light brush of his lips against hers, and then, with a barely audible sigh, he released her.

'Does that help to make amends?'

His blue eyes were full of cool amusement, and Thea knew he was toying with her feelings, testing her for reactions to his technique. Her own eyes blazed with indignation.

'Should it?' she flared. 'Is that how you always reward or punish your secretaries?' She wanted to go on and say that, if so, it was no wonder he lost them so quickly . . . or perhaps had to get rid of them, since lying adoring at his feet might make it difficult to carry out their secretarial duties, but she had the sense to keep the latter comments to herself. Her own heart was still beating with surprised excitement and increased with sudden apprehension as she saw the cornflower-blue of his eyes turn to hardened steel.

She met his gaze bravely, but her teeth gripped at one corner of her lip to stop a sudden tremor.

'Have you been listening to gossip, Miss Lawson?' he asked silkily.

Thea flushed. 'Of course not.' This whole thing was getting out of hand, and she wished now that she hadn't allowed her temper to get the better of her. But, even as caution urged her to retract and make whatever peace she could with him, honesty drove her on. 'But that doesn't mean there isn't any.'

He snorted briefly. 'And there's no smoke without fire, eh?'

'I didn't say that.' He was putting words into her mouth, shaming her into remembering that Rita had said something along those lines. 'Besides, I like to make up my mind.'

'I'm glad to hear it, Miss Lawson.' The steely glint had gone, to be replaced by narrow-eyed mockery. 'I'd hate to think I was wrong about you.'

His fingers tightened on her shoulders and Thea stiffened, her heart pounding fiercely in sudden palpitating anticipation of what was to come next, and wondering if it would be punishment or reward.

'To return to your original question,' he went on smoothly, 'it depends on how good or how bad the particular secretary has been. If you feel my offering doesn't fully make amends, I could always make up the difference.'

His head dipped threateningly.

Thea shied from him. 'That won't be necessary, Mr Clayburn.'

She knew he could hear the panic in her voice, see it
in her eyes, feel the electric tension of her body as he
held her captive. If he kissed her again, or drew her
into an embrace, she would never again be able to
pretend indifference to him.

The rattle of trolley wheels along the corridor broke
the deadlock, and Thea sighed with relief as Matthew
Clayburn's hold on her was released.

'Ah! Here comes the coffee,' he said, adding *sotto
voce*, as Maria's ample rear pushed open the door into
the small kitchen, 'The cavalry has arrived, Miss
Lawson.'

How Thea got through the rest of the meeting was a
mystery, and she was in no mood for Rita's probing
questions when they met in the staff restaurant for
lunch.

In answer to Rita's query as to how her first
morning had gone, she simply shrugged her
shoulders.

'At the moment I'm punch drunk,' she said,
reaching gratefully for her coffee, 'so please don't ask
me.'

'That bad, huh?' Rita snorted inelegantly. 'Well,
don't say I didn't warn you.'

Thea grinned ruefully. 'I know, I know . . . I told
you so,' she chanted, and then set her face grimly.
'But I'm not going to balk at the first hurdle. From
now on, things can only get better.'

'Do you reckon?' Rita said scornfully, her sharp
brown eyes searching Thea's face. 'I think you're
seeing stars, all right, but not because of any boxing
bout. I've seen that look before on the faces of other
females unlucky enough to be around Matthew
Clayburn. It's the look they get before he gobbles

them up and spits them out.'

A dark flush spread up Thea's smooth throat. 'Rita! For heaven's sake, don't be ridiculous. I've only been Matthew Clayburn's secretary for one morning.'

'That's long enough,' Rita insisted doggedly. 'Especially for someone as naïve as you, Thea. He'll get to you, as he has to all the others, and once you're interested he'll drop you like a hot brick and you'll be out of a job.'

'Rita!' Thea said furiously, suddenly remembering Matthew Clayburn's gibe about listening to gossip. 'You may think I'm unsophisticated, but I do know a bit about the grapevine. Stories get passed around and everyone adds their own little bit. They end up being ninety-nine per cent imagination, and I don't intend to sit here listening to tall stories.'

'There you are,' Rita crowed triumphantly. 'Already you're defending him, pulling the wool over your own eyes.' She leaned across the table and pushed Thea's head to the right. 'See that blonde at the table near to the door? That's the last secretary who worked for Matthew Clayburn. If you want it from the horse's mouth . . . what he's really like . . . spend ten minutes listening to Muriel.'

Despite herself, Thea found herself appraising the girl who sat looking sullenly into space, a cigarette between nail-varnished fingers. She was certainly a pretty girl, Thea acknowledged, with a strange pang, and the pert, rather pointed face would undoubtedly be attractive to a susceptible male. And Matthew Clayburn was very much a male, though Thea guessed his susceptibility would always be of the calculated kind.

His handsome face sprang to mind, as he'd coldly

accused her of prejudging him. She'd denied it, and
yet here she was speculating about his response to a
pretty blonde, amazed at the knife-thrust of jealousy
such speculation brought.

She tore her eyes away, bringing them back to
Rita's smugly smiling face.

'Thank you, Rita. But I prefer to make my own
judgement of a person's character,' she said bitingly.
'And, if you don't mind, I'd rather not have this
discussion again. Whatever Matthew Clayburn is,
he's my employer, and as such he deserves my
loyalty.'

Rita's smile faded. 'Is that what you call it?' She
widened her brown eyes in astonishment. 'I call it
masochism.' Seeing the wooden set of Thea's face, she
added in tight fury, 'Oh, suit yourself. I was only
trying to help you. I'm wasting my time, though,
aren't I? You're too far gone already for my help or
anybody else's. You must be his fastest conquest yet.'
She stood up and looked down pityingly at Thea.
'Well, don't expect me to be around later, when
you're picking up the pieces.'

'There aren't going to be any pieces,' Thea
muttered fiercely at Rita's retreating back.

Her words were almost a prayer, a vow, to which
she hoped she would be strong enough to adhere.
Rita's thrust about her being the quickest to fall
rankled hurtfully, and strengthened her determination
to resist her own foolish senses. And the comment
about her being out of a job if she was foolish enough
to fall for Matthew Clayburn struck an answering
chord within her own mind, making her aware of the
tightrope she would have to walk until she could
establish her position with him.

She regretted the row with Rita. If she'd been less

het up, she might have handled her friend more diplomatically and saved herself the trouble of patching up their quarrel. Rita had been a good friend to her since she'd started with the Trust nine months ago, and she knew that, despite her rough and ready methods of tackling any problem, she did it from a warm and caring heart.

Thea sat wearily, picking at the food on her plate and trying to put the events of the morning into some kind of perspective.

Unable to help herself, she stole another glance at the blonde who sat alone, her food untouched before her. Suddenly the wide china-blue eyes slewed in her direction and caught Thea in a cold stare. Mesmerised, Thea stared back, watching the girl's full lips curl contemptuously at the corner.

Thea turned away hastily. Despite the contempt, she had sensed the hurt in the depths of those icy blue eyes and felt pity. If it was true, and the poor girl had fallen for Matthew Clayburn and then been rejected . . . how she must have suffered, and how he would have despised her for suffering!

The more she thought about the rather strange encounter in the kitchen, the more she became convinced that Matthew Clayburn had been submitting her to some kind of test. Was he trying to discover the strength of her commitment to the job? Were her credentials for the job supposed to include a resistance to his undeniable charm? And had she passed?

If she had, then it had been by the skin of her teeth, she told herself grimly, remembering the uncontrollable flare of excitement his brief kiss had brought. From now on, she would take care to keep as far from him physically as was sensibly possible, and keep

her fingers crossed that he hadn't seen beneath her
rigid control.

It was a relief to find on her return to the office that
he hadn't come back from lunch. He'd gone out with
the crowd of men from the meeting, his hand on the
elbow of Mike Donovan, his mind obviously
engrossed in what he was saying, because he hadn't
spared her even the briefest of glances as he left the
office. She hadn't known whether to be relieved or
indignant.

When he did return, well into the afternoon, he
nodded a brief acknowledgement before going into his
room and shutting the door.

Thea had a number of questions she wanted to put
to him about the notes from the meeting, but couldn't
bring herself to disturb him until after four-thirty,
when the mail would have to be signed if it was to
catch the post.

When she finally managed to knock on his door and
enter, he lifted a bland face to hers.

'Ah, Miss Lawson! Come in. Come in.'

Thea advanced somewhat warily. 'I've brought the
mail for signature and the notes from this morning's
meeting. I've typed up some queries on the bits I'm
not sure about.'

'Good. Put them here and I'll see to them in a
moment.' He cleared a space among the paperwork on
his desk and looked up at her as she hastily deposited
the folders and stepped back. His hand had collided
briefly with hers and she'd all but snatched it
away.

'Relax. I don't bite.' He smiled mildly. 'Not unless
specifically requested, that is.'

Thea folded her lips and fought the flush that
threatened to rise to her cheeks. If she'd thought that

her initiation by fire had been accomplished this morning in the kitchen, she was obviously mistaken. He was apparently still bent on testing her responses.

Adjusting her position on the see-saw of his moods was going to be more difficult than she had thought, and she stiffened her resolve not to weaken, but it was hard to keep a cool head when those amazing eyes were twinkling mockingly at her, watching her as a cat watches a mouse, prodding it into escape before sinking its wicked claws. Well, she wasn't going to run.

'Thank you for that reassurance, Mr Clayburn,' she said coolly, though her knees seemed to be about to buckle. 'If you could sign the mail quickly, I'll have time to put it up and take it down to the post-room before I leave.'

The twinkle disappeared and a frown lowered his brows. 'Still in a hurry to get away, Miss Lawson? Another date, perhaps, or is it the same lucky man you're in a rush to see?' His voice held a sharp edge of disapproval.

This time, Thea was unable to stop the guilty flood of colour stinging to her cheeks.

'I'm in no particular hurry, Mr Clayburn,' she said defensively. 'But the hours are eight-thirty to five-thirty, and unless you have something urgent you'd like me to stay on for, I might as well leave on time. I would like to catch my usual train. The next one is an hour later and doesn't run through to my stop.'

He studied her for long seconds, his narrowed gaze holding her defensive one for what seemed an age before he spoke softly. 'And if I said I had something important that I needed you to do . . . you would stay on?'

Thea blinked, while her mind tried to find a footing

on this obviously slippery ground.

'If it was something that important,' she responded, at last, 'yes, I would of course stay.' She moved uncomfortably as he went on looking at her, his expression unreadable. 'Are you asking me to stay?'

He moved suddenly, drawing the folders she had given him towards him.

'Not tonight. But you do understand that there will be times when it will be necessary? I think I made it clear that the job must come first.'

'Yes, you did,' Thea murmured. 'Perfectly clear.'

He wasn't looking at her now as he took up his pen and poised it over the first letter. 'If these are all right, I won't be needing anything more for now.'

She stood by awkwardly as he quickly scanned through the letters, appending his signature to each when he'd satisfied himself they were correct, giving a silent sigh of relief as he approved the last one and looked up.

'An excellent start, Miss Lawson,' he said at last 'Keep it up and we'll get along fine.'

She left dead on five-thirty, passing Linda Prosser, who was on her way in. She gave Thea a superior smile.

'The end of your first day, Miss Lawson. I hope you enjoyed it.'

Thea knew she hoped nothing of the sort, but answered the cool smile with one of her own.

'Very much, thank you, Miss Prosser. Did you want something?'

'Nothing you can help me with.' The grey eyes were hard with malice. 'It's Mr Clayburn I want to see. Is he still about?'

Without waiting for an answer, she swept across the room to the door of the inner office.

'Matthew!' Thea heard her exclaim. 'I've a bit of luck . . . two tickets for the theatre tomorrow. I thought you might like . . .'

Thea left without hearing Matthew Clayburn's answer to the dulcet invitation, seething with indignation and another more painful emotion she refused to identify.

So it was 'Matthew' outside of working hours, Thea thought grimly. It was apparently all right for *him* to have a social life and to fraternise with female staff. Well, he certainly had cosmopolitan tastes, she added sardonically, comparing the fluffy prettiness of the little blonde secretary with the tall handsomeness of the personnel officer. She wished him luck with the latter. He'd need it.

Mike Donovan turned up one afternoon the following week, asking for Matthew, and Thea had to tell him that he'd been away all that day at a meeting.

Mike sat easily on one corner of her desk and grinned at her.

'I expect you're glad of the lull in the tempest.'

Thea smiled. 'You certainly seem to know Mr Clayburn very well.'

In actual fact, she hadn't seen all that much of her employer for the last few days, and when he had put in an appearance he'd seemed hardly to be aware of her, spending most of his time with his head buried in a mass of papers to do with a new scheme the Trust was being asked to finance in Morocco.

'But of course.' Mike grinned. 'We're like that.' He showed her two fingers of his hand pressed tightly together, and Thea laughed.

'Rather you than me,' she replied facetiously, knowing she lied. The thought of being that close to

Matthew Clayburn was doing strange things to her insides.

Mike's grin widened and he leaned conspiratorially across her desk. 'Talking of togetherness, I was hoping you and I might get to know one another a little better.' He lifted blond brows coaxingly. 'I'm at a loose end tonight. How about you and I stepping out?'

Before Thea had time to formulate her refusal, an icy voice cut in.

'Enticing though that invitation might be, Mike, it's not one Miss Lawson is able to accept. I'm afraid I have plans for her myself this evening.'

He strode into the room, his face an unreadable mask.

Thea squirmed. He seemed to have an uncanny knack of arriving at the wrong moment. She eyed him anxiously, wondering if he'd heard her facetious remark. This was the second time she'd come close to being caught out in making a critical remark about him, and she wished she would learn to guard her tongue more closely when she was with Mike.

Mike had coloured faintly, Thea noted, as he grinned rather guardedly into Matthew's closed face.

'Sorry,' he muttered, lifting his hand in a gesture of surrender. 'I wouldn't want to tread on your toes, Matt.'

A blue laser beam shafted between them.

'I'm sure you wouldn't. And don't worry, I can tie your loose end for you.' He put his case on Thea's desk and took out a file of papers. 'Here are my notes on the Morocco proposition.' He offered them to Mike. 'Read them through and let me have your suggestions.' A cold smile curled one corner of his mouth. 'And I'd like them first thing in the morning.'

'I'll do my best.' Mike gave him a disarming smile.

Thea's embarrassment had faded, and in its place was a mounting anger. How dared he be so high-handed? He had treated Mike like a naughty boy caught out in a misdemeanour and, while she understood Mike's reluctance to stand up for himself on a relatively unimportant issue, she couldn't help wishing he'd shown more spirit.

He gave her an apologetic shrug of his shoulder and a surreptitious wink as he turned to leave.

'Mike,' she called, and he stopped to look back. 'Thank you for the invitation,' she said sweetly. 'I would love to come another time. You will ask me again, won't you?'

'Yes. Yes, of course.' He shifted uncomfortably and his eyes went to Matthew Clayburn's hard, watchful face. 'Some time maybe when you're not so busy.'

He left hurriedly, leaving behind an electric atmosphere.

'I'm sorry if I've broken up a budding romance, Miss Lawson,' Matthew Clayburn said as soon as the door closed behind Mike, 'but I've rather a lot of notes I want typed up . . . that's if it isn't too inconvenient for you to stay on.'

Thea boiled with fury. Ignoring the barbed implication, she launched into her attack.

'Not so much inconvenient as very short notice,' she blazed. 'And, if you don't mind, in future I'd prefer to make my own excuses for turning down an invitation.'

He stared coldly into her flushed face. 'I didn't see any point in Mike's being allowed to get any wrong ideas about you. You haven't time to indulge in playful flirtations.'

Thea stared back, astounded. 'Surely that's for me to decide? When you asked for commitment,' she said jerkily, trying to keep the raw anger out of her voice, 'I didn't think you meant I had to become a nun. Everyone, no matter how busy, needs a little relaxation. Even you.' Despite her attempts at control, she spat the last two words at him and rushed on before she could stop herself. 'By the way, how did you enjoy the theatre with Miss Prosser?'

She watched his face darken, the blue eyes narrow to a dangerous glitter, and felt a tremor of apprehension. Had she gone too far? And, even worse, had she revealed to his astute intelligence the green emotion that had given birth to her challenge?

In the next instant, she was surprised to see his face relax and the familar, heart-melting, slow smile curve his lips.

'I might have. But unfortunately I was too busy to take Linda up on her kind offer.' The smile reached his eyes in twinkling mockery. 'You see, I practise what I preach, and always put business before pleasure.'

She should have felt fortunate that he had relaxed his hostility; instead she was filled with a burning desire to get even with him.

'How virtuous,' she said scathingly, incensed beyond caution. 'Unfortunately, not everyone can live up to your high ideals.'

'I'm not concerned with *everyone*, Miss Lawson,' he said silkily. 'Only with you. Tell me, in what area do you feel you might fall short?' He put his hands on her desk and leaned towards her. 'What temptation might you find irresistible?'

He was towering over her, pinning her with his probing gaze, and she stood up, hoping to remove his advantage. It was a mistake she was later to regret. Swiftly, he came around her desk and took hold of her shoulders.

'If it's flirtation you want, it might be less time-consuming to find it closer to home.'

Thea bravely fought the flooding excitement his nearness brought, and threw back her head to glare up at him.

'With you?' she said contemptuously. 'I'm sure you'd be good at office flirtation, Mr Clayburn. After all, you've had enough practice.'

The suddenly savage expression on his lean face shook Thea's courage, and she flinched as his fingers bit deep into the soft skin of her upper arms.

'Is that what "they" say about me, Miss Lawson?' he gritted, pulling her closer as she tried to wrench away. 'You seem to be fascinated by gossip, and I'd hate to disappoint your expectations.'

In the next instant his mouth fastened on hers, while his arms slid around her to hold her more securely to his tightly muscled chest. Her small, startled cry of protest was smothered by the fierce possession of his lips, which plundered her own in exultant pleasure. Instinctively she fought him, but the strength of his arms easily overcame her resistance and, as she ceased to struggle, his hands began to move the length of her spine, arousing a searing response it was impossible to disguise. Her body quivered and, with a faint murmur, he gathered her closer.

His kiss deepened, fierceness giving way to persuasion; his hands were creating eddies of sensation which stole her breath and set her heart beating wildly.

Thea was close to panic. It would be easy, so easy,

to let go, to lose herself to the pulsating delight which was filling her body, to give way to the urgent need of her own hands to explore him in the way his had begun to explore her.

Her body was sinking into a whirlpool of sensation, but her mind fought desperately on. She needed this job and, if she was going to be able to carry on doing it, she couldn't afford to lose the battle she was waging now.

With desperate strength, she pushed against him, managing at last to force a little space between them. His lips lifted from hers momentarily, enough for her to speak.

'Let me go, damn you!' Her voice, a harsh whisper, held a fierce determination and Thea felt his hold slacken.

Taking advantage of this leeway, she wrenched herself out of his embrace and faced him, her bosom heaving as she fought to control her breath.

She had expected to see a cool, cynical expression on his face and was startled to realise that he was faintly flushed, his brilliant eyes a little dazed, and his breathing as ragged as her own.

'And what did that prove?' she asked defiantly.

For an eternity of seconds, he went on looking at her, and Thea knew that, despite her final rejection of him, his effect on her must be displayed clearly in the bruised softness of her lips, the still dewy wideness of her eyes and the swift rise and fall of her breast.

The movement of his chest had steadied and the anticipated cynical smile thinned the firm contours of his lips. But the cynicism seemed, in some curious way, to be directed inwards, towards himself, rather than outwards, to Thea.

'That I'm a fool . . . I think.'

The unexpected answer robbed Thea of words, and she watched in silent confusion as he rubbed a hand across his eyes as though to clear his vision.

When he straightened, his face was almost impersonal.

'I don't think you need stay on, after all, Miss Lawson. The meeting notes can wait until the morning, and then it will be . . .' he paused and Thea found herself holding her breath ' . . . business as usual.'

CHAPTER THREE

SOMEHOW or another, Thea had managed to survive the first few weeks as Matthew Clayburn's secretary. He hadn't touched her since the incident with Mike and, as the work built up, she'd seen less and less of him. He seemed to be almost constantly in motion.

Strangely, despite being a relief, his absences from the office left Thea with a strange restless feeling and she found her eyes lifting hopefully each time the outer door opened, which it did very often throughout the day.

Mike called in occasionally. They chatted easily enough, but he didn't seem inclined to repeat his invitation to go out, which, in a way, was a further relief. In another way, of course, it left Thea burning with resentment, since it seemed that Matthew Clayburn's displeasure discounted any attraction Mike might feel towards her. Her employer had won that battle.

Mike did, however, risk a few playful compliments, which lifted Thea's spirts, but in no way helped fill the peculiarly empty space she felt around her when Matthew wasn't there.

And yet, when he *was* there, he had her running about, more often than not seething with indignation at his barked orders and total lack of interest in her welfare. Since her first morning, he had given her no quarter, expecting her to exhibit an almost clairvoyant anticipation of his needs.

But the first month's cheque had mollified her a

little. After all, she wasn't working for his appreciation nor for his consideration, but solely for the money, and that had been gratifying. There was even enough to allow a mild splurge on one or two much needed additions to her wardrobe.

Thea had planned to spend Saturday shopping alone, but a painful foot had taken Edith Lawson off to the chiropodist, so it was either abandon the idea or take Leon with her.

She was tempted to ring Rita, to see if she'd like to go along and give a second opinion, but thought better of it. They had coffee together and occasionally lunch, when Thea could get away from the office to take it, but the atmosphere between them remained strained.

In the end, she'd taken Leon in his pushchair and walked. The day was warm and sunny and the little boy was enjoying his ride out. It was a fair walk into town but, dressed in a light cotton dress and a pair of comfortable sandals, Thea found the exercise pleasant.

She'd gone in early, before the usual weekend crush, and managed to buy herself a couple of skirts with little difficulty, but had to spend rather more time searching out blouses to suit. Leon was, with every justification, becoming fretful by the time she finally decided on her last purchase, and Thea herself was feeling a little ragged at the edges. The store was becoming hot and stuffy, and they were both glad to emerge at last into the fresh air and a light, cooling breeze.

Thea was standing at a crossing, waiting for the lights to change, when she saw, on the other side of the road, a familiar figure. It was only a fleeting glimpse of a slim form, moving among the press of people, but Thea had no doubt.

'Melissa!' she called, waving a hand for attention.

A face turned briefly in her direction and then was lost in the crowd.

'Melissa!' she called again, more loudly this time, and almost without thinking stepped out on to the crossing, with the pushchair before her.

There was a screech of brakes, and hands were dragging her back. Somehow, a man on a bicycle had grabbed hold of the pushchair, pulling it to safety, and Thea was falling backwards as her heel caught against the kerb. The blow to her head against the light stanchion knocked her almost senseless, and with a sick feeling she lay, fighting to retain consciousness.

'Leon . . . what's happened to Leon?' Her voice was thick with panic.

An arm was about her shoulder, her throbbing head held to a comfortable bosom.

'He's all right, my dear,' came a soothing female voice. 'Your baby's safe, don't fret.'

Relief was quickly swamped by shame. Her carelessness had almost killed them both . . . and all because she'd thought she'd seen her sister. But she was no longer sure. The girl had vanished so quickly.

Nausea caught in Thea's throat, but she swallowed it down and tried to struggle to her feet. Other hands helped her up, and there was Leon, miraculously unhurt and seemingly undisturbed by his hair-raising experience, still strapped firmly into his pushchair. Her parcels were scattered on the pavement and people were picking them up for her, thrusting them into her nerveless fingers.

'You're terribly white, dear. Do you think you'll be all right?' The owner of the soothing voice remained, as others, the drama over, drifted away. 'Would you like me to find you a taxi?'

Thea, shaking from head to foot, found it painful to nod her head. 'Yes, please.'

'That won't be necessary.' A deep male voice spoke commandingly from behind, and Thea winced as she tried to turn her head. A large hand gripped her elbow and she looked up dizzily into the familiar cornflower-blue eyes, which registered frowning disapproval.

'My car is close, Miss Lawson. I'd better take you home.'

Incredibly, he was supporting her with one arm and wheeling the pushchair with his free hand. Thea, clutching her parcels, mumbled her thanks to her kind lady helper and allowed herself to be led away to where a sleek, low car was parked at the kerb.

Her head was beginning to clear a little, and though it ached abominably she felt some strength beginning to return to her trembling limbs.

'Where did you spring from, Mr Clayburn?' Thea asked him dazedly. He seemed able to materialise behind her at the most inopportune moments.

His smile was without humour. 'From hell, Miss Lawson.'

Thea's eyes widened, and for a startled moment she thought she actually looked for horns and a tail.

'I don't think that's funny,' she said thickly.

'Neither do I. In fact, it would have been far from funny for me to have to spend the rest of my life remembering that I had run over and killed my own secretary and an innocent child.'

Thea's eyes fell and her teeth bit sharply into her lower lip.

'I'm sorry. I didn't realise it was your car . . .' She stopped, unable to go on. The thought of what had almost happened to all three of them was overwhelming.

'Yes. Well, fortunately, all is relatively well. So shall we get into my car?'

'I . . . I don't want to put you to further trouble, Mr Clayburn.' She gripped tightly on her lower lip to keep it from quivering. 'I think I can manage by myself now.'

He gave an exasperated sigh. 'I'm parked on double yellow lines, Miss Lawson, and while admittedly I don't have to count the pennies, I do hate throwing good money away on unnecessary parking fines.'

He was opening up the door, almost pushing her into the back seat. Despite her protest, Thea was grateful to find herself seated in safe comfort and amazed to see Matthew Clayburn unstrapping Leon and lifting him up into his arms, hooking the little boy deftly on to one hip as he folded the pushchair and laid it at her feet. 'You'll have to hold your child. I'm afraid I'm not equipped to carry children safely.'

Thea took Leon on to her lap and would have explained that he wasn't her child, but Matthew Clayburn was walking around to the driving seat. She could see his profile, and his expression at that moment looked anything but pleased. He was probably annoyed at having his Saturday morning disrupted by her careless accident, she thought, as she sat back into her seat, hugging Leon close for comfort . . . though whose comfort she wasn't quite sure.

'What's your address?' His voice was curt.

Thea told him, and, receiving a silent nod, found herself wishing heartily that she'd stayed at home, or at least that she'd been more careful and not caused an accident.

She sat silently as the big car wove in and out of the traffic, her heart thudding unevenly at the thought of how easily the baby might have been killed. She, was convinced now that she'd been mistaken in thinking that girl had been Melissa. Of course it couldn't have been her sister. The girl had heard her call, looked her way, but hadn't stopped. If it had been Melissa, she would have stopped, wouldn't she?'

Thea sighed, deciding it was useless to speculate. If it was Melissa, then sooner or later she would turn up at the house. She was surprised at the inner tension that thought aroused.

The car was turning into her street and Matthew Clayburn looked back at Thea briefly.

'Let me know when we reach your house.'

'Yes, of course,' Thea murmured, colouring as his eyes caught hers in the driving mirror. His were hard and surprisingly hostile, and she looked hastily away. She was still feeling the effects of shock and knew she was in no condition to challenge his attitude.

'Here,' she said, as the car drew close to the house. 'Please stop here.'

He halted the car at the kerb and got out to open the rear door for his passengers. He took Leon from Thea and shook out the pushchair before depositing the little boy into it and fastening the strap. He seemed quite at home with babies. Thea's fuddled brain registered the surprising fact as she edged herself out of the door.

His cool gaze was appraising the little house, and Thea was glad she'd spent an evening in the week attending to the garden.

'Is there someone at home to look after you?' he asked curtly.

Thea nodded painfully. 'There should be, by now.' Edith would have been back ages. 'So I won't need to trouble you any further.'

It seemed such an intimate scene, standing beside

him on the pavement, with his hand supporting her beneath her elbow, and the other on the handle of the pushchair. They might have been a family back home from a Saturday morning shopping expedition.

The silly thought added to Thea's embarrassment, and she wanted even more for him to go away.

She looked up at him and groaned inwardly. His mouth was clamped in a tight, hard line. He was obviously still furious.

'Your husband?' he queried, deceptively soft. 'Will he be worried? Should I explain?'

'What?' Thea exclaimed, startled by his assumption. 'Oh, no. I'm not married. I live with my aunt.'

His mouth twisted cynically. 'Well, that's something you haven't lied about, at least.'

Shaken, Thea stared at him, wishing her head would clear so that she could understand what he was saying. 'I haven't lied to you about anything.'

'No?' His brows rose. 'You told me you had no ties, no responsibilities. Doesn't a child count to you as either one or both?'

Sudden colour suffused Thea's pale face. She'd been too shaken by their narrow escape to remember that she hadn't told him about Leon. She hadn't lied, she silently defended, but simply hadn't told him the whole truth. Perhaps she should have done.

'In the n-normal way . . . yes.' Thea was dismayed to find herself stuttering. 'But my aunt takes care of Leon for me.'

He smiled unpleasantly. 'I see. And you obviously don't believe that's a job for the child's mother?'

Thea felt anger chasing out her remorse. 'As a mater of fact, I do . . .' she began heatedly, and then stopped as her body began to shake.

He noticed and his arms slipped about her waist, supporting her against him.

'Come on. Let's get you both inside,' he said. 'We can continue this discussion at a more opportune time.'

Thea stopped walking. Taking a deep steadying breath, she shook off his arm and glared up at him.

'No. We'll finish it now,' she said firmly. 'Firstly, I'm sorry I wasn't as completely honest as I might have been about my circumstances, but I needed the job and I needed the money. In the second place, Leon doesn't make any difference to my ability to do the job, and I have no problems about having him cared for while I'm at work. Lastly, I'd like to go on working for you, but if you want to sack me then it's entirely up to you. But whichever way you decide, I've no intention of discussing my private concerns with you.'

She could tell by his face that she had overstepped the bounds, but in her present state she felt she didn't care. In a way, it was a relief to have things out in the open like this. If he kept her on, then it would be in full knowledge of her circumstances. There would be no need for subterfuge on her part, nor for him to make snide remarks about an impatient lover when he asked her to work on.

But her mouth was dry with tension as the silence went on, and his eyes seemed locked into hers, probing painfully for more secrets. She had none and so let him go on looking.

He spoke at last. 'In two weeks' time, I will be going to an important meeting in Morocco. I had planned to take my secretary. How would you feel about that?'

Thea licked her lips, as her heart began to thud. 'That would be no problem.'

His eyes went to Leon, who was beginning to wriggle about in his pushchair.

'The little one?' His brows rose questioningly.

'He's used to being with my aunt. They're both perfectly happy.'

He shook his head and then shrugged.

'As you say, that's your business . . . as long as it doesn't interfere with mine.'

'It won't.' Thea assured him, hoping that she spoke the truth.

He reached out and touched the back of her head, his fingers sliding almost tenderly through the thick fall of her hair. She wanted to pull away, to escape the sudden shattering desire to lean on him, to feel the comfort of his embrace.

'Have that swelling seen to by a doctor,' he ordered curtly.

Thea nodded silently, miserably aware that he was protecting his own interests. It would be very inconvenient for him to have his secretary out of action now.

'Don't worry. I'll be at the office on Monday morning,' she said tightly. 'I'm sorry about the accident and about wasting so much of your day.'

He nodded with cool acceptance of her apology. 'You're sure you don't want me to see you into the house?'

'No, thanks.' The front curtains were moving and Thea could see her aunt's face peering out. 'I . . . we'll . . . both be all right now.'

Edith Lawson's face was full of suppressed excitement as she met Thea in the hall.

'Who was that incredibly handsome man?'

Thea took Leon from the pushchair and thrust him into Edith's arms.

'You've fallen already, have you?' said Thea drily. 'It seems everybody does.' She folded the pushchair and put it in the cupboard beneath the stairs. 'That's Matthew Clayburn.'

'Your new boss?' Edith's eyes shone brightly. 'Oh, Thea! And he brought you home!'

Thea laughed hollowly. 'Purely by accident . . . literally.'

She told her aunt about the incident and watched the excitement fade from her blue eyes and her cheeks grow pale. She took Leon into the living-room and began to examine him feverishly.

Satisfied that there were no injuries to the child, she turned her attention to Thea.

'Were you hurt?'

'Just a bump on the head.' Thea fingered her scalp gingerly and remembered, with a renewed thrill, that Matthew had done the same, his fingers lingering on the silky smoothness of her hair. The memory brought a strange ache.

Edith tried to insist that Thea see a doctor, but she resisted. 'It's only a bump. Besides, the surgery will be closed by now. Don't worry,' she added, seeing her aunt's anxious face, 'I'm sure I'll survive.'

Edith had to be content with persuading her niece to put an ice pack over the lump, and they sat drinking tea together while Leon took his afternoon nap.

'What I can't help wondering is—was that Melissa?' Thea mused. 'But it can't have been, can it, or she would have come home. Surely she would want to see Leon?'

But Thea knew there was no 'of course' where Melissa was concerned. She sighed. 'She's so spoilt. And I can't help blaming myself. I should have been

firmer with her . . . made her stay at home and face up
to her responsibilities . . . look after Leon.'

As Matthew had said, that was a job for his mother
. . . and Melissa was his mother.

'You mustn't blame yourself,' Edith said
comfortingly. 'You did your best after Ray and
Margaret died . . . more than your best . . . but the
spoiling had already been done.'

Thea's brows wrinkled as she recalled that last
awful scene with her sister.

'You've never wanted me to succeed, have you?'
Melissa had spat the words at Thea, her pretty face
distorted with fury. 'You'd much rather I was like you
. . . happy to rot in the same old rut all my life. Well, I
won't.' She'd tossed her multicoloured hair and glared
at Thea vindictively. 'If you'd let me go to drama
school when I wanted, I'd have made it by now.'

'I couldn't afford it,' Thea had protested. 'There
was no money.'

'Hah!' Melissa had stormed. 'No money for drama
school, but you were willing to find it for a course in
boring secretarial college.'

'That course was only for a year, Melissa, and God
knows it would have been hard enough to find the
money for that. It was the best I could do.'

'Your best . . . but not mine.' Melissa had held up
her neat head proudly. 'I've got talent and, one way or
another, I'm going to prove it . . . to you and to . . .
to. . .' She'd stopped there, her face flushed, her eyes
gleaming with uncharacteristic tears.

Despite her own hurt at Melissa's barbed words,
Thea had felt compassion. It was true, Melissa did
have acting talent, but whether it was enough, Thea
felt she was in no position to judge. Melissa had
always shone in the school plays, but there was a big

difference between amateur status and professional, and the competition was daunting.

'I know you can act, Melissa,' she'd said placatingly. 'But it's a hard world out there and most people never make it.'

'I'll make it.' Melissa's lip had curled contemptuously. 'And when I do, I'll make you grovel.'

The following morning she'd gone, leaving Leon behind, and a cryptic note to Thea. 'You'll see.'

Well, that had been a year ago, and neither Thea nor Edith had seen anything of Melissa since. At first, they'd received the odd postcard from the different towns in which she was playing, but soon even those stopped arriving.

'Stop worrying, Thea.' Edith broke into her thoughts. 'Things will work out for the best . . . I'm sure they will.'

Thea kissed her aunt's cheek.

'Oh, Edith!' she said softly. 'Where would I be without you?'

CHAPTER FOUR

THEA still had a headache on Monday, but there was no way she was going to let the Saturday morning incident keep her away from work.

Matthew Clayburn was in before her and Thea plucked up the courage to beard the lion in his den.

'Good morning.'

He looked up and his blue eyes appraised her coolly. 'Good morning, Miss Lawson. How do you feel? Any problems?'

Thea shook her head. 'No. None.'

He nodded. 'And Leon?'

She had a momentary vision of him with the little boy slung easily on his hip as he folded the pushchair. The vision was somehow moving and Thea swallowed. On Saturday, he'd been wearing jeans and a casual sweater and, apart from the familiar grim expression, he'd seemed light years away from this smartly groomed and dark suited man.

It seemed strange to hear Leon's name flow so easily from his lips, especially since he was still being so correct with her own name. But what else could he have called the child? she asked herself irritably.

'He's fine. No after-effects as far as I can tell.'

'Good.' He nodded and turned back to his paperwork, his interest in the subject obviously exhausted.

Thea heaved a sigh of relief. It was good not to have to keep Leon secret any more, but she didn't want to foster Matthew Clayburn's interest in the little boy.

He obviously disapproved of working mothers, and even more of unmarried mothers. Of course, that wasn't her own situation, but it might as well have been, since she had the full responsibility of providing for Leon.

Looking down at his engrossed expression, she didn't feel inclined to put him right on that score. Anyway, it wasn't really his business. As long as she did her job to his satisfaction, her private life was of no concern to him.

He looked up suddenly and caught her studying him.

'Have I grown horns, Miss Lawson?'

Thea flushed. She'd actually been thinking what a dangerously handsome devil he was. Could the man read her mind?

'Not that I can see,' she muttered in an attempt at flippancy, before moving away. 'I'll get my notebook if you're ready for dictation.'

The amusement in his blue eyes burned a hole in Thea's retreating back.

She was relieved to see no hint of it on her return.

'I'll give you a list of the preparations I want you to make for the staff meeting next Friday,' he said brusquely. 'The first half of the evening will be a serious affair. I want to put everyone in the picture about the new scheme. Afterwards, a buffet will be provided so that everyone can mingle and discuss their own part in the venture. There'll be food and wine, but not enough of the latter to encourage anyone to over-indulge. I want some sensible results from the evening.'

Thea had to buy a new dress, one that would perform the dual functions required of it: formal enough for the meeting and attractive enough for the buffet later. She was lucky to find just what she was looking for in a hurried lunch-time foray to a small nearby boutique.

Edith thought the delicate shade of turquoise brought out the colour of Thea's large and rather unusual eyes.

'You look stunning, dear.'

Thea laughed. 'I love you for being so biased.' But she couldn't help wondering if Matthew Clayburn would agree. He probably wouldn't even notice, she derided silently. All he was concerned about was that the evening should be a success and produce the expected results of stimulating interest and a will to participate in his precious new scheme. It was his own brainchild and he'd invested heavily of time and effort in its inception.

On Friday, Thea stood beside him at the door into the lecture-room. The buffet had been prepared in the large visitors' lounge next door.

She'd used the office en suite bathroom to shower and change and had been secretly pleased at the expression on Matthew Clayburn's face when she'd finally emerged in her new dress, having carefully dried and arranged her hair and taken extra pains with her light make-up. Perhaps the dress did do something for her, after all, she'd thought, as she saw the undoubted gleam of interest in his eyes. But her pleasure had been short-lived.

'I'm not sure that dress won't prove too distracting, Miss Lawson,' he'd said, a heavy frown between his dark brows. 'I want these people to keep their minds on what I'm saying.'

Thea had flushed. So he hadn't been referring to himself when he'd spoken of distraction. To him, she was probably simply an attractively covered piece of furniture. At any rate, she'd felt sat on.

'Oh, I'm sure I'll be no competition against your fascination, Mr Clayburn,' she'd said, rather more acidly then she'd intended.

He'd laughed, his blue eyes smiling mockingly into hers. 'So! You *have* noticed. I was beginning to wonder.'

And what had he meant by that?

Thea had no time to wonder further, as his mood changed and he led her away, with hurried irritation, to perform her duties.

Rita came in with Muriel, Matthew's previous secretary, and Thea wondered uneasily if they had become close friends. There was no reason why they shouldn't, of course, but Rita had been in a peculiar kind of mood since she'd quarrelled with Thea, and Muriel, even though Thea hadn't spoken to her, had seemed hostile right from the start.

Tom Griffiths came shortly afterwards, diverting Thea's attention away from the girls.

'How are you doing?' he asked Thea. 'Any regrets?'

Thea shook her head. How could she answer that question honestly? There were times when she wished she'd never even heard of Matthew Clayburn . . . times when she longed for the relative calm of her old job with Tom.

'Ask me in six months' time,' she said now, adding with a wry smile, 'If I'm still around then.'

'I'll do that.'

'Miss Lawson,' Matthew Clayburn's voice interrupted them, hard with irritation, 'that file of papers on the scheme. Where is it?'

Thea started. 'I put it with the other files on your desk. Aren't they all together?'

'All but that one. Go back to the office and get it.'

His voice was harsh, dictatorial, with nothing of the humour of half an hour ago.

Thea bit her lip and, with a worried nod at Tom, she went rushing off along the corridor. Her pulse was racing. This was the third file that had gone missing in a week. By the law of averages, they should have turned up by now, but they hadn't. If this one had disappeared in the same way, Matthew would probably explode. He'd been fairly philosophical about the loss of the others, but this one held the notes of his speech as well as statistical reports. It was absolutely vital.

But, though she searched every inch of her own office and Matthew's, the file was nowhere to be seen. In a panic, she even skimmed through the filing cabinets, knowing it wouldn't be there. In her mind's eye was a clear picture of her own hands putting that file on top of all the others, so that Matthew could put his hand on the information it contained with absolute ease.

'Thea, for God's sake—have you found it yet?'

'No.' She was shaking from head to foot. 'I've looked everywhere, but it was a waste of time because I remember specifically putting that file on top of the others.'

'Well, it isn't there now. I've had a good look around. Damn!' One fist beat forcefully into the other. 'Is it too much to expect a little efficiency?'

Thea felt like arguing against the unfairness of it, but held back. At least he hadn't thrown the other two lost files up in her face.

His eyes flicked to the slim gold watch on his brown wrist. 'I should have started ten minutes ago.'

Thea's eyes shone with threatening tears. 'Matthew, I'm so sorry. What can I do?' She wrung her hands.

'What can I say?'

'Nothing.' His mouth set grimly. 'But I'll have plenty to say to you later.' He eyed her coldly. 'And that's the first time you've called me Matthew.'

In the event, he managed very well, ad libbing through the parts of his speech he couldn't remember without his written prompts. He skirted around the subject of statistics and promised everyone directly involved would have a copy of the relevant figures on Monday. Fortunately, they were on computer and it would be relatively simple to reproduce the file. Even so, it was a calamity Matthew could have done without.

No one seemed to notice the steely glint in his eyes as they occasionally met Thea's, nor the way she sat with her hands clasped, white-knuckled, in her lap, That was, except for Muriel. Her eyes remained coolly on Thea for most of the time Matthew was speaking, making her feel uncomfortable. She was pale, Thea noted, and her eyes shone with a strange kind of fervour.

It was a relief, probably to Matthew as much as to herself, when the meeting broke up and everyone adjourned to the room next door for something to eat and drink. The atmosphere was cordial and most people seemed to have something enthusiastic to say to someone else about the scheme.

Thea circulated, advising everyone to help themselves. Matthew was at the centre of a group which was still deep in discussion. Mike was there and he met Thea's still unhappy gaze. He winked and she gave him a wan smile.

Matthew intercepted it and frowned. 'Thea, come over here.'

She moved towards him, wondering when had *he*

started using *her* first name?

As she drew near, he took hold of her upper arm. 'This is Tony Amhurst.' He introduced her to a tall, swarthy man of about fifty, who enveloped her hand in his large one. 'He's the man you'll be liaising with on the Morocco deal.'

Thea smiled. It was the first time he'd mentioned Morocco since the morning of the accident, and in the hectic rush of the past week she'd given it no thought. She was tempted to ask him if he still intended to take her with him. After the fiasco of the lost files, it was possible, she supposed, that he might be having second thoughts.

'I suppose you have made the necessary arrangements for your . . . er . . . responsibilities to be taken care of while we're away?' he said now, pausing pointedly to ensure she understood his meaning.

'Yes. Of course.'

Thea let out a faint sigh. So he did still intend to take her. She didn't know whether to be happy or anxious. A week or so in his company, in such close proximity for twenty-four hours of the day, wasn't going to be any picnic, she warned herself, but decided in the end that she was happy to be going.

'Tony will fill you in on the paperwork we'll need to take,' Matthew said. His eyes narrowed on Thea's. 'When they're ready, they'd better be put under lock and key until the last minute. We can't risk any of them going astray.'

She might have known he wasn't going to let her off the hook on the subject, but for the life of her, she couldn't even begin to understand what had happened to the files.

'I'll take the utmost care that it doesn't,' she said, meeting his gaze steadily.

The party had begun to break up before Thea could snatch a minute to have a quiet glass of wine and something to eat. Rita had left some time ago, but Muriel was still there, clutching a bottle and a long-stemmed glass, looking a little unsteady on her feet. Every so often, she broke into a shrill little giggle.

People were beginning to look at her, and Thea wondered, a little apprehensively, if she was expected to do anything about it. Before she could decide, Muriel had made her way across the room to where Thea was sitting alone.

'And here's the new secretary,' she said unevenly, and Thea had no doubt now that Muriel was drunk. 'None other than wonder bloody woman, Thea Lawson.'

Thea's eyes slewed quickly in search of Matthew, but he was, fortunately, at the other side of the room, still engrossed in conversation with a small group of men.

'Hello, Muriel,' she said with as calm a smile as she could manage. 'Enjoying yourself?'

Muriel's smile was crooked and malevolently lewd. 'Not half as much as you'll be enjoying yourself in Morocco, I dare say.' She leaned over Thea, waving the half-empty wine bottle aloft. 'I'll drink to that.' She tried, unsuccessfully, to pour some into her glass and failed. Thea moved her skirt out of the way of stray drops.

'Don't you think you've had enough, Muriel?' she said in a low voice, trying to keep out an edge of panic. 'Would you like me to call you a taxi?'

'You can call me what you like,' the girl said thickly. 'And I shall call you a whore. Matthew Clayburn's latest whore!' Her voice was rising shrilly. 'Don't forget to pack pretty frillies when you go away together. He just *loves* black lingerie.'

'I think we've been entertained enough for now, thank you, Muriel.' Matthew Clayburn's voice was low and hard with menace. 'It's time you went home.'

Muriel turned to him, her lips smeared damply, and smiling in a ghastly travesty of coy invitation.

'Yes, Matthew darling. Please do take me home. It wouldn't be the first time, would it?' She swayed unsteadily. 'But first I'd like to christen your venture.' She lifted the bottle of wine. 'I name this ship *Betrayed Lady the Millionth.*' She giggled shrilly. 'And God bless all who . . . sail in her . . .'

As Matthew lunged for her, she turned the bottle upside-down pouring the wine over Thea's head.

With a startled gasp, Thea jumped up, just as Matthew grasped Muriel's wrist, sending the bottle flying from her hand. It caught Thea a hard blow to the temple. The last thing she saw was Matthew's savage face looming over her before she lost consciousness.

The earth seemed to be moving beneath Thea's back and there was a low hum in her ear which was difficult to define. Her eyes were closed, the lids weighted with lead. It was a struggle to open them. She moved and groaned as pain shot through her temple.

'Stay still, Thea.' A command from a long way off, which had Thea struggling again to orientate herself.

'Where am I?' she muttered thickly.

'On the back seat of my car,' Matthew's voice was gruff. 'Lie still for a while. You've had a nasty blow on the head.'

A strange feeling of *déjà vu* overcame Thea. She was lying in Matthew Clayburn's car with a throbbing pain in her head. Had she been run over after all? And where was Leon? She hadn't known she'd voiced her fear aloud.

'Leon is a home with your aunt, presumably,' Matthew said. 'And this time, I'll make sure you see a doctor.'

The whirlpool inside her head had began to recede, leaving behind small eddies of heat and cold and a desire to vomit.

'I feel sick,' she murmured miserably, putting a hand to where her head ached the worst. Her fingers made contact with a gash in the skin and the thick stickiness of blood. The shock cleared her head and she put up another exploratory hand.

'My hair is soaking wet and so are my clothes,' she said in amazement. 'And where are you taking me?'

'We're nearly home,' Matthew said gently, as though soothing a child. 'Ask questions later.'

'But I can't go home in this . . . mess! Aunt Edith will have a fit.'

'That's what I thought, so I'm taking you to my place.'

Thea tried again to sit up and this time she managed it. Matthew's dark head was directly in front of her. He turned briefly and met the anxious confusion of her gaze.

He smiled reassuringly. 'Don't worry. It's not much further to go.'

She wanted to protest that there was no way she wanted to be alone with him in his home, but vertigo was threatening again and she sank back down on to the seat. Slowly, memory returned, making her groan. It all seemed like some kind of lurid nightmare. Muriel had accused her of being Matthew's mistress in front of a host of interested listeners. How would she ever be able to face those people again?

'Here we are!'

The car pulled off into a driveway and came to a halt before a large detached house. Thea roused herself to look out of the window at the attractive building, which had obviously been converted into a number of discreetly expensive flats.

The car door opened and Matthew was there, indicating his intent of helping her out. She refused the offer of his hand.

'I . . . can manage,' she said shakily. But she couldn't. As soon as she tried to stand, her knees buckled weakly, so that he was forced to support her against him.

'Wonderful!' he snorted, a soft cynical sound. 'Now perhaps you'll stop being a fool.'

He swept her up into his arms, holding her easily as he kicked the door of the car shut with his foot. Thea's head, which seemed to weigh a hundred-weight, sank on to his broad shoulder, nestling against the powerful column of his throat, where she could hear, in a detached sort of way, the powerful rhythms of his heart. She knew she ought not to allow him to do this, but was full of a strange kind of contentment. In his arms, she felt safe, secure, and suddenly very drowsy; she wished she could just fall asleep.

'Wake up, Thea. Help me get this dress off.'

She was lying down again on something firm and comfortable, she didn't want to move.

A hand came beneath her head, lifting her, sliding the dress from her shoulders, moving lower to distentangle the wet, clinging material from her hips. Unaccountably, she seemed to be naked, a cool, wet cloth caressing her skin, a soft towel patting her gently dry. Then something cool and silky was being pulled over her head, making her wince as it caught against her sore temple.

The shock of the sudden pain brought her more fully to her senses. Her eyes opened and focused.

Matthew hovered above her, his brilliant eyes shadowed with anxiety. Was it he who had taken her clothes off? Thea wondered, her heart quickening its beat, sending the blood rushing to clear her head.

'Thea, try to stay awake. I don't know whether you're supposed to sleep with concussion. The doctor will be here in a few moments.' He touched her head, moving the damp, heavy hair away from her forehead. 'How do you feel?'

'Fine,' Thea said, in obvious contradiction of the truth.

'Oh, yes, fine.' He sighed with a gentle exasperation. 'This is all we need now. For you to have a second bump on the head, when you haven't even got over the first.'

She frowned, the movement starting a fresh trickle of blood on her temple. 'What do you mean?'

He put a damp cloth to her head, patting it gently. 'Don't worry about it now. I dare say we'll find those files eventually. 'It's not too important.'

Thea sat up, a little dizzily, but now fully aware of what was happening.

'But it *is* important, Mr Clayburn. If you're suggesting I've been mislaying files because of a bump on the head, you're mistaken. The first two files I've been keeping an open mind about, though if they had been mislaid they should have turned up by now. But the one for the meeting today I'm quite definite I put it on top of all the others. I'm certain I did.'

'Then where is it?' he asked, in faint irritation.

'I don't know. But I intend to find out.' She chewed fretfully at her lip. 'I don't think I'm quite ready yet for the men in white coats and their strait-jacket.'

He laughed shortly. 'I haven't suggested you are.
'We'll talk about it some other time, when you're
feeling better.'

He was humouring her and Thea felt angry. If she'd
wondered at his initial mild acceptance of the lost
files, she now understood. He'd been making
allowances for her, hoping her apparent slip-up was
the fault of her accident, though secretly fearing he
might simply have found himself yet another
inefficient secretary. It wasn't something she intended
to let pass, but knew she was in no condition to
pursue the matter now.

'I'm feeling better already. And I think I should go
home.' Almost for the first time, she realised that she
was in bed, wearing nothing but a pretty white silk
nightdress.

'Wh . . . where are my clothes?'

'In the washing machine,' he answered drily. 'Then
they'll go into the dryer to be ready for ironing. My
housekeeper is taking care of it now.'

His housekeeper! So there was somebody else in the
house. She sighed with relief, and even found time to
hope that the woman knew what she was about. She
couldn't afford to ruin a new dress. It had cost a small
fortune. Would she be reimbursed if it was ruined?
Thea pulled herself up. Her mind seemed to be
rambling.

'I see. I'm very grateful. Please thank her for me
and for . . . this . . .' She flushed, her fingers pleating
uncomfortably at the silk nightdress. 'Also, of course,
for . . .'

His smile was ironic. 'It was I who gave my services
in that respect, my dear Thea. I thought you might
prefer me as the lesser of two evils, since my
housekeeper is also a male.'

Thea's flush deepened, remembering the sensation of being washed all over by a gentle hand. No doubt he had relished having her so completely in his power.

And if his housekeeper was a man, then to whom did the nightdress belong? Wild horses wouldn't have dragged the burning question from her.

She heard the thin peal of a bell.

'That'll be the doctor,' Matthew said. 'I'll go and let him in.'

What about the housekeeper? Thea wondered. Wasn't it part of his duties to answer the door? Or were male housekeepers above that sort of thing? Her eyes roamed around the room. Whatever he didn't do, she thought laconically, his housework was beyond reproach. Every surface gleamed, and the sheets within which she lay were crisp and scented.

The nightdress she wore too had the same subtle perfume, and she wondered anew at the owner. As though in answer to her unspoken query, she was suddenly aware of the picture-frame on the small round table close to the bed. It was double-sided, propped open like a book, with a photograph in each side. One of a laughing, dark-haired girl, the other of two children, a boy and a girl of about six and four respectively.

Thea's eyes widened in startled surprise. The children had the same bright cornflower-blue eyes and thick dark hair. Matthew's children? Her insides turned uncomfortably. No one had ever mentioned that Matthew Clayburn had a wife.

She had a sudden image of Matthew with Leon slung very confidently on one hip, and remembered her surprise at his competence. It was obvious now that it came from experience—with his own children.

Her cheeks were suddenly very hot. Was she lying in *their* bed, wearing *his wife's* nightdress? And it wasn't black, she thought, a little hysterically, recalling Muriel's taunt about Matthew's preferences.

Was there some psychological significance here? The purity of white for his wife, the sophistication and devilry of black for his mistresses. The thought was too monstrous. She couldn't believe even Matthew Clayburn was capable of such duplicity.

He could be divorced, of course. It did happen, even to men like Matthew Clayburn. But somehow she didn't think so.

Her eyes went reluctantly back to the photograph of the woman. She was good-looking, with intelligent brown eyes and a smile which said she knew exactly what she wanted. Not the kind of woman it would be easy to fool. How well did she know her husband? Thea wondered. Perhaps well enough to let him go his own way, with reservations. There were marriages like that, she knew.

Thea shuddered with revulsion and sat up. The too-rapid movement brought the blood singing dizzily into her head and she sank back again with a groan. Her urge to get out of the bed and discard the intimate garment she was wearing would have to be postponed. She had nothing, as yet, to replace it.

Matthew came back with the doctor and Thea heard him apologising for his delay in coming. Apparently, he was a locum standing in for Matthew's family doctor, and he'd had difficulty in finding his way.

The doctor was young and rather attractive, and Thea saw the frown on Matthew's face as he made his examination, his hands moving competently over her body.

'It was a blow on the head, Doctor,' he said drily.

Thea thought she detected an edge to the words, and wondered a little nervously if he was becoming impatient with the whole business.

'Yes. I can see that. A very nasty gash, I'm afraid, although I think you'll get by without having stitches.'

As he pressed the crown and back of her head with gentle fingers, he touched the previous swelling which had gone down considerably but not entirely disappeared.

Thea winced.

'Were you hurt here, too, Mrs Clayburn?'

Thea started in embarrassment and, as the colour flooded her cheeks, her eyes flew expectantly to Matthew's. His mouth was twitching at the corners with wry amusement, but he made no comment. He was leaving her to explain her own predicament.

'Oh, but I'm not . . .'

'Another accident, I'm afraid, Doctor,' Matthew cut in smoothly. 'Less than a week ago she tripped on the kerb. I'm still rather concerned about that.'

Thea glared at him. How dared he let that absurd mistake go uncorrected? If anything, he was compounding it with his misleading talk of concern.

'Hmm. Well, it seems to be healing up quite nicely. No lasting effects, I'm sure.'

'Not even impaired concentration, Doctor? Things being mislaid, perhaps?'

Thea fumed. She'd been wrong. He *was* concerned. But only to prove himself right.

The doctor nodded. 'Maybe. But it'll pass. You must try to take better care of your wife, Mr Clayburn. She seems somewhat accident-prone at the moment. Keep a close eye on her for the next week or so; make her rest. And don't hesitate to ring the surgery if you're worried.'

'I'll take your advice, Doctor, on both counts, you can be sure.'

When he came back from seeing the doctor out, Thea was out of bed and standing shakily alongside, trying to decide if the trembling was weakness or temper.

'If that's your idea of a joke, Mr Clayburn, then I'm afraid I don't think it very funny.'

Ignoring her outburst, he picked her up and deposited her unceremoniously back on to the bed.

'The doctor ordered rest. You heard him tell me to keep on eye on you. Perhaps you ought to stay the night to be on the safe side.'

'Thank you, but that won't be necessary,' she said stormily. 'And I'd be glad if you'd ring the surgery on Monday and explain the misunderstanding.'

He nodded calmly. 'Of course I'll do so, if you wish. But aren't you afraid of your reputation? After all, the doctor did visit you in my house, in bed, wearing nothing but a flimsy nightdress. I might add that he seemed to find you rather fetching, notwithstanding the fact that he thought you were married to me. All in all, I might have a little difficulty convincing them of my version of the truth.'

'Given your reputation, you mean?'

His eyes narrowed. 'You seem to know more about that than I.'

'And your own doctor might know a little more about you than a locum.'

He nodded amicably. 'I'd say there was an outside chance that he might. Should I be worried about that?'

'Oh! You're impossible!' Thea's chest heaved with frustration. 'And I've never felt so humiliated.'

He raised dark brows in mock astonishment.

'Do you mean you didn't enjoy the experience of being Mrs Clayburn?'

Thea's insides were shaking, a mixture of rage and disbelief that he could have brought her here in the circumstances and be so uncaring of the consequences. Had he no shame?

'Isn't that a question you ought to ask the real Mrs Clayburn?'

He frowned, studying her flushed face with implied incomprehension.

'Do you mean my mother? I should think she's quite resigned to the name after all these years.'

Thea bit her lip, refusing to let him see her unaccountable distress. The blow on the head seemed to have scrambled her emotions as much as her brains. The pain she was feeling had nothing to do with the gash on her head.

'You know precisely what I mean.' She pointed at the photographs on the table. 'Your wife . . . and presumably your children. Do you mean your mother doesn't know she's a grandmother?'

His eyes widened for a moment in what seemed genuine surprise, and then he smiled as though enjoying a private joke.

'Oh, no. She's quite aware that she has grand-children. She rather revels in it, as a matter of fact; only she seems to imagine they belong to my sister.'

'Your sister?' Thea flushed scarlet. Completely thrown, she found it difficult to speak for some time. 'I'm afraid I thought . . . the eyes are so like . . .'

She stumbled to a halt, wanting nothing more than to bury her burning face in the pillow.

'I'm sorry,' she mumbled agonisedly.

Matthew shrugged. 'A natural mistake in the

circumstances, I suppose.' He picked up the photographs and studied them fondly, the hard planes of his face softening. Thea thought she had never seen him look so handsome. 'They do look rather like me, don't they? As you say, it's the eyes. A characteristic of the Clayburn side of the family. Angela follows my mother.'

'They're lovely,' Thea said, and then bit her lip as she saw his expression. 'The children, I mean.'

'Of course,' he said suavely. 'I didn't think you meant my eyes, my dear Thea.'

His eyes sought hers mockingly, and Thea felt the familiar drowning sensation: floated weightless in brilliant blue seas.

'Does she live with you . . . your sister?' Her voice sounded faint and breathless. The question was too personal, but she was desperate to take her mind away from the subtle promise of ecstasy his eyes had conveyed.

He laughed, releasing her gaze, and Thea let out her pent-up breath.

'Good heavens, no! Angela's too strong-minded a baggage to live with anyone. And that's the problem.'

Thea's insides tautened. A second embarrassingly wrong assumption in a matter of minutes. But if the nightdress wasn't Angela's, then . . .

Her fingers plucked unconsciously at the soft white silk.

'Ah!' Matthew said in the manner of having made a discovery. 'The nightdress.'

He came disturbingly close, hooking a casual finger beneath her chin so that she couldn't avoid his direct gaze.

'I wonder what lurid pictures you're conjuring up in that beautiful head of yours, Thea.' His voice was

as smooth as the silk she wore, and sent ripples of
sensation surging through her sensitised nerves. And
she wished he'd go back to calling her Miss Lawson.
'If I knew, would I be flattered or furious?'

Thea swallowed convulsively. 'I don't know. Do
you think I could have my clothes now, please? I have
to go home.'

'Home, as they say, is where the heart is.' With both
hands, he smoothed the damp hair from her cheeks
and, with infinite care, from her injured temple. 'Who
gives your heart a home, my lovely?'

A tremor ran the length of her body. It was hard to
speak over the lump which had risen inexplicably in
her throat. And what could she say? That life, and the
few men with whom she had shared a kiss, had left her
heart untouched?

Before she could even formulate a reply, his lips
lowered gently over hers. A kiss without passion,
sweetly exploring, almost hesitant, drawing from her
a tremulous response. Her mouth softened, and her
hand of its own volition reached shyly out to touch his
hard chest, her fingers creeping up to touch his cheek.

He shuddered and, without lifting his lips from
hers, gathered her closely against him, deepening his
kiss, sending lightning flashes of excitement bursting
through Thea's desperately reeling senses.

Some small corner of her mind retained its sanity,
warning her that she would pay for this brief ecstasy,
its hopeless voice drowned by the crashing beat of her
heart.

His hand moved against her, stroking the curve of
her spine, her pliant waist and upwards towards her
breasts. With a feeling of reaching the edge of an
abyss, she put her hand sharply over his, willing him
to stop before it was too late.

At that contact, his body jerked as though with sudden shock. His head lifted and he shook himself as though wakening from a dream. He took her shoulders and put her gently from him.

'Perhaps, after all, you're right, Miss Lawson. It's time I took you home.' His voice was low and ragged and strangely angry.

Abruptly he left her, presumably to fetch her clothes, his handsome face stern, his back held rigidly.

Thea stared after him, filled with hurt and a puzzled resentment. The touch of his mouth still vibrated against her lips, tingled through her senses, the memory of his hands still generating heat enough to melt an iceberg, and yet he'd looked at her, before stalking off, as though it was *she* who'd turned *his* world upside-down.

She was back to being Miss Lawson again and firmly in her place, and at some level she was glad of it.

Smouldering resentment fanned into flame. Was this the technique he used with all of his secretaries? Filling their days with heights and depths, hopes and desperation? How easy it was for him, she thought furiously. How easy she had *made* it for him. She was filled with self-disgust.

'I think I'm beginning to feel sorry for poor Muriel,' she said aloud.

'What a strange thing to say. Particularly since you're presently suffering the consequences of *poor* Muriel's vicious stupidity.'

Thea stiffened with shock. She hadn't heard him return. He seemed always to be sneaking up on her.

'Perhaps I understand that, too,' she said stubbornly. 'Do you treat all your secretaries to the same hot and cold treatment?'

He frowned darkly. 'I treat my secretaries as they deserve. In Muriel's case, I admit I made a mistake. I should have fired her instead of allowing her to move to another department. It's a mistake I intend to remedy.'

'You're going to fire her? My God! You're heartless!'

'I prefer to call it practical. The girl is useless.'

'Useless? Or madly in love with you?'

He shrugged. 'I doubt the latter. In any event, I neither asked for nor wanted her love.'

Thea's mouth twisted bitterly. 'But you weren't above taking it when offered.'

His lips thinned to a hard line. 'How easily you believe the worst of me, my dear Miss Lawson. Since you obviously prefer Muriel's version of our relationship . . . her word to mine . . . I won't seek to disillusion you.'

Thea bit her lip. 'I've never discussed you with Muriel . . . so it's not a question of preferring her word to yours.'

'I'm glad to hear it. Now perhaps we can dispense with the tedious subject of Muriel. As far as I'm concerned, she simply didn't do the job I paid her for.'

Icy cold fingers of apprehension crept up Thea's spine as she remembered the missing files.

'Then I shall have to make sure I do.'

'Thank you, Miss Lawson. That's all I ask.'

Please help me remember that, Thea prayed feverishly, pushing away the memory of his kiss. Whatever the kiss had been, he now obviously regretted his indiscretion.

He turned as a knock fell on the door.

'That will be Pearson with your clothes. Thank God

for a competent, uncomplicated man about the house.
Get dressed and I'll drive you home.'

Seated beside the silent, grim-faced man as the car
wound its way through the evening traffic, Thea
fought her confusion. Her head was sore and she felt
vaguely sick, but whether from the blow or her inner
turmoil, she couldn't tell.

She wished fiercely that this evening hadn't
happened. Just when she had begun to establish some
kind of working rapport with Matthew Clayburn, the
incident with Muriel had blown up to change
everything. He might be able to pretend he had never
kissed her, never held her in his arms, but she
couldn't. Every time she looked into those incredible
eyes, looked at the firm shapely mouth, she would
remember.

'How do you feel?'

Matthew's question intruded into her thoughts,
bringing a little warmth at his concern.

'I . . . I'm not sure,' she said shakily. 'A bit groggy, I
think.'

He grimaced. 'Of course, this would have to happen
just before Morocco. Do you think you'll be fit
enough to go?'

So much for his concern, Thea thought cynically.
As always, he was worried about himself.

'I'm sure I will,' she said more firmly. 'I have a
whole week to get over it.'

He grunted. 'It's going to be a hectic week of
planning and packing. Hardly a rest cure.'

Thea bit her lip. What could she say to that? Did he
expect her to predict how she would feel a week from
now?

'I'm sure I'll be all right.'

He relapsed back into silence, a heavy frown descending on his brow.

'And then there's the question of the child,' he said, a minute later. 'How can you be so sure he won't miss his mother?'

Thea started. 'He's used to it,' she said, without thinking.

His frown deepened alarmingly. 'And that makes it all right does it?'

'No. It doesn't make it all right,' she hit back angrily. 'It's just the way things are for the moment, and there's not a lot I can do about it.'

'I know,' he cut in sardonically, 'you have to make a living.'

'Yes, I do. My living and his living and my aunt's living. And it isn't easy.'

'I'm sure it's not.' Had his voice softened? 'But what about the father? Didn't you think to ask him to contribute? If not, then it's about time you did.'

Thea put a hand to her head, which had begun to throb. 'I agree,' she said harshly. 'And if I knew who he was . . .'

She stopped because she'd suddenly remembered he thought Leon was hers. 'What I mean is . . .'

His face was blank with astonishment. 'Do you mean you don't know who Leon's father is? My God! Could he have been any one of a number?'

The contempt in his voice cut Thea to the quick and made her furious. He was using the same old double bind. He seduced every woman in sight and that made him a rake. If a woman did the same, it made her a whore. Despite her anger, she was tempted to explain, but then, she thought, none of this was his damned business.

'No. And if you don't mind, I'd rather not go on

discussing it. If you're worried about Morocco, don't be. Aunt Edith will cope. Just forget about Leon.'

'As you seem quite able to do.'

Thea let the gibe pass. She was close to tears of frustration and weakness, but she wouldn't let him see it.

'Back at the house, you complained that your secretaries expect too much of your personal attention. You said all you were interested in was getting the job done. Well, that's all I'm interested in, too. So I'll be glad if, in future, you'd leave my personal affairs to me.' She was trembling with reaction. 'And, by the way, I think it would be better if, in future, you didn't kiss me.'

Thea was aghast. The minute she'd said the words, she wished them unsaid.

He was smiling, but his nostrils looked pinched and white.

'I think that, at least, is something we can both agree on, Miss Lawson.'

CHAPTER FIVE

EDITH reached for a tissue and sneezed.

Thea looked at her anxiously. 'You're not starting a cold, are you?'

That would be all I need, she thought silently, instantly disgusted with herself for her selfish thought.

Edith shook her head. 'No, of course not. I've been dusting. It always makes me sneeze.'

'Are you sure? If you're going to be ill . . .'

'Thea, for heaven's sake, if you don't stop worrying, it's you who is going to be ill.'

'I can't help it. So many things have gone wrong lately, I can't help wondering what's next.'

Edith tutted. 'And that's the way to make things happen. Now, calm down and leave everything to me. Leon and I will be fine.'

Matthew hadn't mentioned Leon again since the night he'd brought Thea home, but his concern had added to her anxiety. This was the first time she had ever had to go away from home and leave Edith to carry the responsibility for Leon alone. Only now was she fully realising that it wouldn't be the last. Was it always going to be as difficult every time to make the break?

She chewed almost frantically at her lip. Perhaps, after all, Matthew had been right. The job needed someone who could give it complete commitment with no ties. As it was, she'd given less and less time and attention to her aunt and to helping around the

89

house, and in addition to everything else now carried that added burden of guilt. Being Matthew Clayburn's secretary seemed to absorb all her energy.

As he'd predicted, the week had been a hectic one and fraught with an electric tension.

Beyond the one cursory assessment each morning, when he asked after her state of health, she might just as well have been a very sophisticated computer . . . there simply to absorb and produce.

It seemed obvious that he was keeping out of her way, barking his instructions mainly through the intercom. Thea told herself it was better that way, especially since she invariably found herself shaking whenever he came too close.

When he did have to speak to her, he avoided looking directly into her eyes, saving her, at least, from the danger of betraying her vulnerability.

Monday morning brought an added trauma. On return from her coffee-break, she found Muriel sitting in one of the visitors' chairs, white-faced and visibly shaking, as she waited for Matthew to call her into his office.

Thea's attempt at speech was greeted with silent hostility and she withdrew with a sigh. Even now, she couldn't help feeling sorry for the girl. She was young, inexperienced and somehow raw; no match for the man who sat stony-faced behind his desk as Thea was, at last, requested to show her in.

Thea heard the low hum of Matthew's voice and five minutes later Muriel emerged hurriedly, her eyes shining with suppressed tears, her chin thrust aggressively forward.

'He won't get away with this!' she hissed furiously at Thea, before slamming the door on her way out.

Matthew made no comment when Thea went in later

to give him his mail.

It was Rita who gave her the news of Muriel's instant dismissal. She'd telephoned Thea to ask if they could have lunch together in the staff restaurant. Thea was relieved to think there might be a thaw in the cold war Rita had been waging, but felt it more likely that Rita was fishing for information.

'I don't know anything about Muriel,' she said as an opening gambit. It was as well to let Rita know she didn't intend to be pumped.

Rita laughed grimly. 'Well, you're the only one who doesn't. It's all over the building that he told her to get out immediately.' To Thea's surprise, Rita didn't blame Matthew. 'There wasn't much else he could do, after Friday's fiasco,' she snorted derisively. 'Only a fool kisses and tells, especially where a man like Matthew Clayburn is concerned.'

Thea stirred her coffee furiously. 'I'm not convinced there were any kisses to tell about, Rita.'

'Oh, come on! Are you still trying to whitewash him? Do you honestly mean to say he hasn't kissed *you* yet?'

Thea crossed her fingers beneath the table. 'That's precisely what I mean to say.'

She held Rita's probing stare calmly, but beneath the surface her insides were running riot. Thank God it wasn't possible for Rita to see the visions that were flashing through her mind. The awful thing was that part of her agreed with Rita. He *had* kissed her, more than once, with devastating effect. And it was foolish to go on trying to convince herself that she was special . . . that he hadn't handed out the same kind of treatment to any of his other secretaries. Was it a question of belief in Matthew Clayburn or an attempt to protect herself from the hurt of acknowledging the truth? But *was* it the truth? her mind argued stubbornly.

Rita's smile was mean. 'Perhaps he's saving you for Morocco. When you're both far away from home, out of sight of curious eyes.'

'Eyes like yours, you mean, Rita?' Thea bit back. 'When are you going to stop pretending you mean well and admit you're just an idle troublemaker?'

Rita heaved with indignation. 'Thea Lawson! If I wasn't your friend, I'd let you stew in your own juice. As it is, you're so blind you need *someone* to point it out to you.'

'If that's the real reason you're interfering,' Thea said breathlessly, 'then you needn't worry. I can take care of myself.'

'That's only what *you* think.' Rita was scornful. 'I wonder if Muriel thought the same.'

It was what Thea wondered, too, in her private moments. Would the same fate await her if she was foolish enough to fall in love with Matthew Clayburn?

Not a very auspicious start to the week, but at least no more files went missing. Thea kept a careful eye on everything, locking drawers and filing cabinets whenever she had to leave her room. It added to the irritations of the day, but at least everything had remained where she'd last left it, which was a point she intended taking up with Matthew at the first appropriate opportunity.

By Friday, she was a bag of nerves. They were travelling on Saturday, late evening, and she still had most of her packing to do. She'd had to go shopping during the lunch hours for things she'd have managed without otherwise. A couple of nightdresses, mere whispers of crisp cotton for the anticipated hot nights, and a light bathrobe, which would double for the beach, if she ever found time to do some sunbathing, which was by no means certain. The itinerary she'd typed up for the various meetings seemed to allow little time for relaxation.

Nevertheless, an evening dress was the next on her list. Long or short? Which would be more appropriate? She had no idea, never having been abroad before, nor ever even having stayed in a hotel. She took advice from the boutique assistant and chose a calf-length cocktail dress of light french navy, which seemed to cling alarmingly to her curves. Thea bit her lip and shook her head.

'Isn't it a bit too revealing?'

But the woman was adamant. 'You look wonderful. Sleek, elegant and sophisticated.'

Oh, well, she couldn't argue that that wasn't exactly how she wanted to look. With Matthew Clayburn for a close companion, she would need some kind of armour . . . a second skin for protection.

She tried hard not to wonder how he would look in light summer clothes. Would he wear short-sleeved shirts revealing muscular, slightly hairy arms? Shorts to show off lean and powerful thighs?

Stop it, Thea, she admonished herself. You'll drive yourself mad.

It was a whole week before Matthew actually spoke to her properly.

She took the mail in for signing at four-thirty on Friday afternoon. He was sitting behind his desk, staring abstractedly out of the window, his dark head silhouetted against the light, his profile still stern and infinitely powerful.

Thea's heart thudded uncomfortably. She still hadn't found the secret of its control.

She coughed for his attention and he started,

swivelling around to look at her. His eyes brightened
and, for a moment, he looked almost pleased to see
her.

'Ah! Miss Lawson! Come and sit down. I'd like a
word with you.'

Thea obeyed, glad to have support for her suddenly
wobbly knees, but not altogether sure she wanted this
confrontation now.

'There hasn't been much time to talk this week.
How are you feeling?'

'Fine,' Thea said. 'Absolutely fine.'

She flushed under his close scrutiny. The blue of
his eyes was brilliant, dazzling her senses, and she
wished he would turn away.

'You look tired. Not surprising in the circumstances, but perhaps you could do with a little
relaxation before the hard work really starts.'

Thea blinked. 'Yes—well, when I've finished my
packing this evening, I'll have a nice relaxing bath.'

His grin flashed whitely.

'I suppose I could give you a hand. I have had some
experience in that direction,' he joked. 'But perhaps
that wouldn't be particularly relaxing for either of us.'

Thea's flush deepened, remembering the sensations
of being washed by him in cool water. Underhand of
him to remind her.

'I think I'd rather manage alone, thanks. If you
could just sign the mail . . .'

'I have two tickets for the theatre tonight, Thea. I
think you should come with me . . . wind down a
little.'

Thea couldn't think of anything less likely to help
her unwind.

'Thank you, but . . .'

'It's an order, Thea. Part of the job. I want you fit

and at your best, and this is the way I choose to do it.'

It seemed a million years ago that she'd first informed him he didn't pay for her time outside the office, but the glitter in his eyes warned her it would be dangerous to remind him again.

'I'll be at your house at seven-thirty. Don't be late.'

Thea was in the grip of an agonising decision. Should she wear the turquoise dress again, or the new one she had bought for Morocco? She didn't really want to wear her new one now. It would seem secondhand by the time she came to wear it abroad. She was tempted to take a fresh look at her accounts, but even if she could afford to buy another dress it would be a last-minute rush before flying tomorrow.

In the end, of course, she had only one choice. To wear her new dress. She felt a subtle thrust of excitement as she remembered the way it had clung to her body. Would Matthew be impressed? How had the shop assistant described her appearance in it? Sleek, elegant, sophisticated. Something like that.

Edith was almost more excited than Thea, making it all the harder for Thea to control her own anticipation. He had ordered her to come with him, but Thea was determined that tonight she would call the rest of the shots.

'Oh, Thea! You look so lovely. How can any man hope to resist you in that dress? It's wicked.'

Thea frowned with sudden doubt.

'Do you think it's too much? Perhaps I should wear my turquoise one, after all?'

'I'll murder you if you do!' Edith was exasperated. 'You were never one to display your talents. You always left that to Melissa.'

'Talking of Melissa,' Thea said, 'I wonder if we're

ever going to hear from her.' She chewed her lip, thinking of what Matthew had said about a child needing its mother. Poor little Leon.

'Don't frown, dear,' Edith admonished. 'It will give you lines.'

And grey hairs, Thea added sardonically. If she had to carry on this battle between her commitment to her job, and her love and loyalty to Leon and her aunt, she would quite definitely be inviting an early old age.

With one half of her mind she wished Melissa would come home and look after Leon; the other half dreaded her sister turning up only to go rushing off again, upsetting Leon and everyone else.

The doorbell rang on the dot of seven-thirty, and Thea despatched Edith to answer it.

'It will give you the chance to have a little private drool,' she teased.

And give me a chance to check my make-up, she told herself, as she rushed upstairs to apply a brush to her already perfect hair.

From Matthew's expression when she descended the stairs a minute or so later, she knew the dress was definitely a mistake. His eyes raked over her and she could tell he was seeing again the figure beneath the clinging material, and there wasn't a lot he would have to recall purely from memory. The quizzical lift of his brows let her know she was right.

'You look stunning.'

Thea shot him a resentful look. She would have let her temper fly if her aunt hadn't been looking from one to the other of them, a certain smile of satisfaction on her face.

A cry from upstairs cut across the tension of the moment.

'That's Leon.' Edith started up the stairs. 'He's

cutting his back teeth and it's making him a bit restless.'

'Why don't you bring him down,' Matthew said, surprising the two women.

'I don't think . . .' Thea began.

'It might distract him a little . . .' Edith said at the same time.

'The play doesn't start until eight-thirty,' Matthew said. 'And I wouldn't mind a cup of coffee.'

Thea went into the kitchen to make him his coffee, and Edith went up to fetch Leon.

As she waited for the kettle to boil, Thea explored her feelings, a confusing mixture of gratification for his interest and anxiety. Why *was* Matthew so interested in Leon?

When she took the coffee through into the living-room, the little boy was sitting on Matthew's knee, looking up at him with owlish curiosity, his large blue eyes solemnly assessing.

'Do I pass muster, old man?' Matthew laughed, and tweaked Leon's nose.

Leon's face broke into a beaming smile and he put up a small hand to clutch Matthew's tie.

Thea put the coffee on the small table.

'You'd better take him, Aunt, before he puts that tie in his mouth,' she warned uneasily.

Matthew grinned.

'It wouldn't be the first time I've been creased and christened,' he said, handing the little boy back to Edith, where he snuggled happily in her arms.

Thea handed Matthew his coffee and felt his fingers lightly brushing hers as he took the cup.

'He seems very content.'

'Oh, he is.' Edith beamed with pride. 'And very bright. Do you know what he did the other day?'

Thea bit her lip as her aunt launched into tales of

Leon's latest escapades. Matthew seemed suitably impressed and amused.

'Don't you think we ought to be going?' she broke in at last. 'We don't want to be late.

Matthew twinkled at her. 'Have I managed to train you into punctuality?'

Thea frowned. 'I was only late once, Mr Clayburn, and that was before your time.'

The 'Mr Clayburn' had slipped out and Thea flushed in confusion as he raised his brows at her in mock surprise.

'I think we might dispense with the formalities for tonight, Miss Lawson. You have my leave to call me Matthew, if I may call you Thea.'

I know what I'd like to call you, Thea fumed, but she only nodded for the benefit of Edith who was smiling again. Asking him into the house hadn't been such a good idea, after all, and she was suddenly anxious to remove him from the vicinity of her aunt and her little nephew.

Edith seemed to have no such reservations. She shook hands warmly with him and Leon waved in friendly farewell as they eventually left the house.

The play was a fairly amusing farce, and Thea found the tension beginning to ease out of her body as she became involved in the light complexities of the plot.

Matthew seemed to be enjoying it too, and when her hand touched his in the heat of laughter, he took it and held it gently. When she realised, she tried surreptitiously to pull her hand away, but his grip tightened slightly, making it impossible. Her body surged with sudden excitement and, despite herself, the contact made her happy. She didn't dare meet his eyes, but turned her attention determinedly back to the play.

It was well into the middle of the first act that the vamp appeared, and Thea's attention suddenly became riveted on the slim blonde.

With her heart pumping madly, she forcefully
retrieved her hand and opened her programme at the
page listing the cast. The actress was Lisa Loreson. For
a moment, she thought her mind must after all be
feeling the effects of her accident, but when the girl
laughed she was suddenly sure. It was Melissa. Melissa
Lawson . . . Lisa Loreson. Melissa had changed her
name!

'Is something wrong?'

'No. No.' Thea struggled to calm her agitation.
'Everything's fine.'

But as soon as the first act was over she found it difficult to contain herself.

'Would you like a drink?' Matthew's brows drew
together as her eyes darted about. 'Are you all right?'

'Yes. I'm sorry, but do you think you could help me
find the dressing-room? There's someone I must speak
to.'

If he was surprised, he hid it very well. Calmly, he
took her elbow and led her around to the rear of the bar
and through a door into a corridor.

'This is the way, if I remember rightly.'

'You've been here before?'

'Yes. Once or twice.'

What was the music hall expression? Thea thought a
little wildly. A stagedoor Johnny. But this wasn't the
music hall. What on earth was wrong with her?

Thea was breathless with anxious anticipation, trying
not to let her mind run to imagining Melissa's reaction
to finding her there. Her sister was unpredictable, to say
the least, and she didn't want a family confrontation
with Matthew alongside her. He'd already been more
closely involved with her family than she would have
liked.

'Well, here we are.'

Matthew drew her to a halt in a corridor of doors. People were milling about in every direction.

'Which member of the cast do you want to see? Actually, I don't think between acts is an ideal time for visiting.'

Thea bit her lip. 'I'm sorry. But I've got to find out if I'm right. I'm looking for my sister. The blonde girl who came on late in the first act. She's calling herself Lisa Loreson, but I'm sure it's Melissa.'

A man who looked like the stage manager was standing close by, ushering people this way and that. Obviously the second act was about to start shortly. Thea rushed across and tugged on his arm.

'Excuse me—I'm looking for Melissa Lawson . . . er . . . Lisa Loreson. Do you know where she is?'

'Dressing-room four. And tell her when you see her she's got less than five minutes.'

Melissa opened the door in answer to Thea's knock. Close to, she was almost unrecognisable. The multi-coloured hair had been bleached to an overall blonde, two or three shades lighter than her own natural colour, but it was well cut and in condition. The make-up was heavily theatrical, but expert. She looked older in a hard, glamorous way.

'Oh, God!' she said, when she saw Thea standing there. 'I was wondering if you'd turn up.'

'Melissa! It really is you. How long have you been in town? Why haven't you come home?'

'Two minutes!' bawled the man from the wings.

'I have to go,' Melissa said. 'Come back at the end of the show if you still want to.'

'Of course I want to,' Thea said tightly. 'Don't you want to ask me about Leon?'

Melissa's face stilled for a second, as though trying to

recall the name. Then, 'Yes. We'll talk about Leon.'

Her eyes flicked beyond Thea's shoulder and she smiled, her face lighting with interest, a cynical, questioning tilt to the corner of her mouth.

Thea turned, following her gaze, to find Matthew standing quietly some little distance behind. Appalled, she realised that for a while she'd forgotten him completely. She opened her mouth to apologise, but his eyes at that moment were on Melissa, and there was a tiny frown puckering between his brows.

'Oh, dear! I'm sorry, Melissa, this is . . .'

'*Ten seconds!*'

Melissa said, 'I've got to go. Introductions later, but I have a feeling your friend and I have already met.'

The rest of the performance was an agony of suspense. The whole of her concentration was on Melissa, and despite her riotous thoughts Thea registered that her sister's performance was both competent and amusing. On one level she felt proud of Melissa, who had, at least, made it this far under her own steam. On another, she worried about the future for them all, and longed to talk to Melissa.

On the odd occasion when she looked at Matthew, she found that he, too, was focusing on her sister, and she wondered what he was thinking. How awful that his planned evening of relaxation should instead have wound Thea up tighter than a drum. In a way, she wished she hadn't found out about Melissa until after she'd come back from Morocco. She had a sneaking suspicion that finding her sister was going to create more problems than it was going to solve.

'I'm sorry, Matthew,' she said contritely, as he again led her down the corridor to the dressing-rooms. 'I hope this hasn't completely spoiled your evening.'

'On the contrary,' he said rather stiffly, 'I've a feeling

it's going to prove rather interesting.'

What did he mean by that? But Thea had no further time to wonder. The atmosphere backstage was high with excitement. The performance had gone well and the audience had been more than receptive. The cast and crew were laughingly congratulating themselves and everyone else, and Melissa was in the middle of an admiring group as Thea drew near.

Melissa, face alight, opened up a space in the circle and drew Thea into it.

'Listen everybody—I'd like to introduce my older sister,' she called, her arm about Thea's shoulder. 'Thea. Without whom none of this might have been possible.'

Thea was startled by this public acknowledgement, and flushed as she became the cynosure of all eyes.

The group laughed and wanted to shake Thea's hand. Her head felt light with all the noise and confusion, but she smiled at the sea of faces.

'And this,' Melissa shouted above the hubbub, 'is Matthew Clayburn.' She stepped forward and thrust her arm through Matthew's. 'Managing director of Principal Trust. Be nice to him,' she added, with a trilling laugh, 'he's the man with all the money.'

Both Melissa and Matthew were swallowed up in the general crush, and it was quite some time before Thea met up with him again. The champagne was beginning to run out and the initial loud excitement had quietened a little to party level, when she saw him moving almost surreptitiously around the edge of the crowd.

She was burning with curiosity about how he and Melissa knew one another. Her sister's attitude to him had been archly proprietorial; Matthew had simply looked uncomfortable and rather annoyed. His face was set and frowning now as he came towards her.

'Have you had enough?' There was a slight edge to his

voice and Thea felt guiltily that she'd dragged him into something he would perhaps have preferred to avoid. But he had, by his own admission, been backstage before, so he must have known what he was letting himself in for. Was that how he'd met Melissa?

'Yes, I have. But I was hoping I might manage a quiet word with Melissa before going.'

Curious as she was about her sister's relationship with Matthew, she had far more urgent issues to sort out with her.

Catching Melissa's eye had been virtually impossible. She seemed to be the centre of attention, for the cast as well as the visitors who'd been invited back for the celebrations, and she was quite obviously loving every minute of it. Thea's rather hesitant efforts to get her attention had been completely ignored.

'I don't like to interrupt her for the moment, but it is important I speak to her.'

Matthew smiled grimly. 'If that's all that's holding us up . . .'

Thea watched him rather uneasily as he penetrated the group surrounding Melissa and expertly disentangled her from her admirers.

She seemed quite happy about it, until she realised that he was leading her towards Thea, and her expression as he withdrew to leave the women together boded ill.

'I'm sorry, Melissa,' Thea said, dismayed by the furious scowl on her sister's face. 'But I must talk to you about Leon.'

'For heaven's sake, Thea, stop calling me Melissa! You'll confuse people. They know me as Lisa. And I can't think about Leon now.'

Thea bit back the angry retort which rose to her lips, and instead managed to speak reasonably.

'I should have thought your son would be the first thing you would think about.'

Melissa's eyes flashed warningly. 'Of course I think about him. But there's a time and place, and this isn't it.' Thea's eyes widened in astonished disbelief, and Melissa went on, her voice rising belligerently, 'This show is the beginning of my career, Thea. Can't you see that? And I've got to give it *everything*. I can't *afford* to divide my attention now.'

'Is that why you ignored me the other day in town?' She didn't say she'd almost killed herself and Leon trying to attract her attention.

Melissa dropped her eyes from Thea's questioning gaze and, for a brief second, Thea thought they darkened with pain.

'I saw you with Leon. I heard you call, but I couldn't have stopped . . . couldn't have looked at him . . .'

'Oh, Melissa!' Thea's voice was soft with understanding. Melissa did care for her son, after all. 'Surely it wouldn't distract you too much just to see him? Why don't you come to the house tomorrow? He's got to get to know his mother some time, and the earlier that is, the better for him . . .'

Melissa's head came up with a jerk, her eyes meeting Thea's fiercely.

'You always know what's best for everyone, don't you, Thea? But more especially for yourself. You're not prepared to help me in the smallest way, are you? You just can't stand the idea that I might be successful.'

Thea's insides churned with bitter anguish. 'That's not true. I've done everything I can for you. You said it yourself, in front of all these people.'

Melissa smiled cynically. 'People say things they don't mean all the time in this business. That's something you learn quite early on.'

'But why say it if you didn't mean it?'

'Because I wanted to feel I had someone behind me . . . someone who cares . . . I wanted to think I wasn't alone.'

Thea touched her arm. 'You're not alone. I care, and Aunt Edith . . . and . . .'

'Leon? Oh, yes! Keep on reminding me!' Her voice was low and venomous. 'You love him so much, you can't wait to dump him back into my lap, can you?'

'That's not true,' she denied, her voice as weak as her knees. 'I do love Leon . . . very much . . . and all I want is for him to be happy . . . safe and secure for the future.'

Melissa laughed harshly. 'And you think the best way to do that is to ruin *my* future?'

All the energy seemed suddenly to have drained from Thea's body. Melissa's lack of understanding, her undeserved animosity, was a brick wall she'd been banging her head against for years . . . too many years. Blindly she stepped back, seeking the support of a wall . . . and found she'd backed up against someone standing directly behind her. A hand came up to hold her arm. She twisted to look up, and saw it was Matthew. He looked down at her for an instant and she felt a strange, flooding relief that he was there.

He turned his narrow-eyed attention to Melissa.

'Forgive me for interfering in what is so obviously a family discussion, but don't you think you're missing the point, Miss . . . er . . . Loreson? Thea doesn't have to justify giving you back your own son. He's your child and therefore your responsibility. How you manage your *career* around that is your business, not your sister's. She has a career of her own to pursue.'

The emphasis on the word career wasn't lost on Melissa. She coloured angrily. 'And whose interests are *you* pursuing? Your own, I'm sure, knowing you. Are you and Thea planning on shacking up together? Is that why you're trying to get rid of Leon?'

Thea gasped, appalled at her sister's ability to viciously twist everything to her advantage.

'Stop it, Melissa!' she said sharply. 'This obviously isn't a good time to talk reasonably. Unfortunately, I'll be abroad with my job for a week starting tomorrow, so I won't be around to sort things out. I wish now that I hadn't come here to talk to you about Leon. I don't want you arriving on the doorstep, upsetting Aunt Edith before I get back.'

'Poor Thea. Would you like me to say I won't, so that you can go off and enjoy yourself without a care?'

'It's not a question of enjoying myself,' Thea returned tightly. 'It's my job.'

She felt Matthew's fingers tighten on her arm and looked up at him.

'I'm sorry. I didn't mean it the way it sounded,' she said. 'I like my job and I was really looking forward to going to Morocco.'

He raised his brows sardonically. 'But, now . . .?'

Thea shook her head, biting on her lip to keep it from quivering. 'I'll go. Nothing's changed. Leon will be fine with Aunt Edith.'

'Not a very satisfactory situation, though, is it?' He frowned darkly. 'As you say, when this trip is over, things will have to be sorted out.'

Thea nodded, her heart as heavy as lead, accepting the inevitability of what he was implying. She couldn't blame him. He'd been perfectly honest about what he wanted most in his new secretary. Absolute commitment, no ties. It was obvious from the grim expression on his face that he felt she had broken trust with him.

His hand dropped from her arm and he moved

restlessly away. 'If you're ready, I suggest we leave.'

'Yes. Yes, of course.' Thea missed the warmth of his hand, the security of him standing behind her.

'I . . . I'll talk to you when I get back home, Melissa.'

'I can't wait,' Melissa said sardonically. 'Perhaps you and I will compare notes. I'll tell you my score if you'll tell me yours.' She shot a meaningful glance at Matthew's stony face, and then smiled at Thea, a dry, humourless smile. 'Enjoy it while you can, Thea dear. You're not the first by a mile . . . and you won't be the last.'

Thea burned with embarrassment and an impotent fury as she struggled against the urge to smack Melissa's malevolent face, aware of Matthew's rigid anger and of the smiles of the curious onlookers who had begun to gather in a group nearby.

'Goodbye, Melissa,' she said in a voice low and hoarse with controlled anger.

Melissa's light laugh followed her as she turned to leave. 'Goodbye, Thea. And thanks for wishing me luck.'

In the car, travelling homeward, Thea struggled with words to express her regret, but as she opened her mouth to begin, Matthew waved a dismissive hand and shook his head.

'Not now.'

Thea's heart sank. This disastrous evening had spoiled everything.

If only she hadn't agreed to come. Or if only she hadn't recognised Melissa and insisted on going back-stage . . . But it was useless to wish away what had already been done.

Seeing Melissa had increased her anxiety rather than alleviating it. She seemed harder, more stubbornly entrenched in her own distorted point of view. Leon's future seemed even more insecure at this moment, since it was impossible to imagine him being happy, or even adequately cared for, by Melissa in her present mood. Unless she changed quite drastically for the better, which seemed unlikely, Thea could foresee a serious battle ensuing, perhaps even a legal battle to keep Leon where he was presently happy, with herself and Edith.

And Melissa, thwarted, could be vicious. Her behaviour tonight had more than adequately confirmed that.

It was still a puzzle as to how and when she had met Matthew. Perhaps later, when they talked about Leon's future, Melissa would tell her, would amplify her insinuations. Knowing her sister, Thea guessed her story would be exaggerated well beyond truth. In any event. Matthew's past was none of her business. And his future would cease to be her concern very shortly if his expression now was any measure of his intentions.

He was obviously furious, his profile cold and remote, his brow dark and furrowed with concentration. The outcome of his deliberations was a foregone conclusion, Thea accepted dismally, and probably fair, in the circumstances. It was both a consolation and a torment to know the axe wouldn't fall immediately. He couldn't sack her now at the last minute. He needed her in Morocco. Once they were back, however, it would be a different story.

She wondered if she would be allowed to have back her old job with Tom Griffiths, but it was a forlorn hope. After the recent fiasco with Muriel, it didn't seem likely he would want any more of his discarded secretaries remaining in the building.

CHAPTER SIX

THEA ran a weary hand through the heavy strands of her hair. They were damp with sweat and her whole body felt sticky and uncomfortable. In the air-conditioned comfort of the hotel boardroom, she had hardly been aware of the heat, but outside, as she crossed the gardens to her own room, it hit her like a searing oven-blast. She eyed the sparkling water of the pool, almost deserted as it neared meal time, as someone stranded in the desert might eye on oasis . . . as salvation.

For the first couple of days, she'd hesitated about using it, afraid she might find Matthew there and be forced to see him in his swimming trunks, muscled body gleaming. It would have been too much. She bothe hoped and dreaded to see him, but he was never there.

Since that ngiht at the theatre, she'd felt a terrible sense of loss, and each day, sitting beside him, while he was stern and withdrawn, she'd had to fight a painful yearning to touch him . . . to make him look at her . . . admit her existence. But his firm body was set like granite, his eyes chips of amazing blue ice.

Thea shivered in spite of the heat as she climbed the steps to her front door.

The hotel was a delight. Each room had been built as a small, dazzlingly white replica of a Moroccan house, completely separate from each other and built on differing levels, which gave the effect of a village.

The interior was on two levels, crossing from the

front door to a beautifully tiled bathroom with a luxurious sunken bath and a separate toilet.

Thea stepped down the two steps into the living area and sank on to her bed—a thick mattress in a handmade wooden box, which was quaint and very comfortable.

But there was no comfort in her heart. Four days had gone by without her catching a glimpse of Matthew beyond the times when she met him in reception for half an hour each evening to receive tomorrow's 'briefing', and then the precious hours when she sat beside him at the meetings, taking notes and trying not to catch fire each time she felt the cold, light touch of his hand which indicated she should record verbatim.

The first evening they'd arrived, she'd worn her turquoise dress and hoped to see him at dinner, but had found her companion was to be Tony Amhurst, the man she's been introduced to at the fateful party. Hollow with disappointment, she'd done her best not to enquire into Matthew's whereabouts, but the question burst from her lips of its own volition.

'Isn't Mr Clayburn dining with us?'

Tony's answer had been disconcerting. 'Otherwise engaged, my dear.' He'd stretched his large mouth in a wide grin and winked knowingly. 'The pressures of big business need a special kind of relaxation. These Moroccans know a thing or two about that.'

Thea's nose wrinkled in a distaste at the obvious implication, and she found herself clenching her nails into her palms. She couldn't see Matthew in that kind of set up, she denied fiercely. And yet, why not? Didn't every occupation have its own special perks?

'And why aren't you included in the arrangements?' she asked, an uncharacteristically waspish note in her voice.

Tony shrugged, still smiling. 'I've been detailed to make sure you don't get any unwelcome offers. I might get quite a few camels for you, I dare say . . . if you were mine to sell and I had somewhere to keep half a dozen camels.'

He shook his head in mock disappointment, and Thea found herself laughing as his face crumpled disarmingly into laugher.

His crack about Matthew's being entertained else-where hadn't been deliberate, she assured herself. He couldn't possibly know the thought of such a thing broke her heart. But she wasn't that transparent, and he would never know if she could help it.

She turned a dazzling smile on him. 'Then I can rely on you to keep me from a fate worse than death.'

His hand touched hers briefly. 'You won't be able to rely on me for a single thing if you go on smiling at me that way.'

Thea felt the heat of his palm against the back of her hand and pulled it sharply away.

'Don't worry, my, dear,' he said reassuringly. 'You're as safe as houses with me. You've got to be, or else . . . ' He made a cutting motion with a broad finger across his throat. 'Orders from above.'

Her brows pulled together in a frown. So, Matthew was still making sure that she formed no distracting alliances. Even though he was probably planning her dismissal immediately on their return, he couldn't keep from exerting his power over her.

She looked away to hide her vexation, and caught the glance of a man seated at a nearby table. A very handsome, dark-skinned man with large, luminous brown eyes glowing his approval of her, flashing very white teeth in a seductive smile.

Thinking of Matthew and full of a sudden rebellion, she answered his glance with a demure half-smile, and his expression lit up with delight.

It was a gesture she was later to regret, for he seemed to materialise from nowhere whenever she chose to appear unaccompanied in public.

She'd learned that he was a doctor from a nearby hospital who lived locally and often took dinner at the hotel.

Somehow he'd persuaded Tony Amhurst to introduce him to Thea, and he was becoming less hesitant with each day that passed. He was there before her at the pool, and she stifled a sigh of irritation as he came towards her. Her mind registered his film-star good looks, wishing she could respond to their allure. But with her heart full of Matthew, every other man faded into insignificance.

'Good evening, Miss Lawson,' he greeted her, his eyes sweeping over her figure in its blue swimsuit. She'd put a light beach robe over, but hadn't tied it, wanting desperately to get some cool air to her body.

She pulled the robe about her now as she shook the long-fingered brown hand he extended to her.

He sat down beside her on the adjacent lounger, and for the first time she noticed that he was also in swimming trunks, surprisingly brief, and showing off his dark, muscled torso to advantage.

Thea thought about the inequality of the sexes in Morocco. The men often wore western suits and frequented the restaurants and lounge bars of the hotels, whereas the women were still enclosed in volumes of material with only their eyes visible. When passing strangers in the streets, they averted their eyes and dropped their heads even further into the enveloping folds. She wondered how they stood the heat.

She was longing to plunge into the cool water of the pool, but was reluctant to remove her robe in front of the admiring doctor.

'I was wondering, Miss Lawson,' he broke into her train of thought, making her start guiltily, 'would you be interested to see the hospital? It would be an honour for me to escort you there. You will see how much progress we have made.'

A refusal rose automatically to her lips. Her first inner response was that she didn't want to encourage him; her second was that Matthew would disapprove, and anger kindled into flame.

What right did he have to dictate to her about what she did in her own time? In a little while, nothing she did would be his business, so she might as well start practising for her freedom.

Yet still she hesitated, knowing on some inner level that it would be foolhardy to accept. She was a stranger in an exotic and still mysterious land. An acceptance might be a casual, friendly gesture to her, but it could mean something entirely different to a Moroccan in his society. Tantamount, perhaps, to offering herself to him.

His large eyes fixed on hers like some small boy pleading for a treat. She wavered, and he saw and understood.

'Please. It would mean so much to me,' he cajoled her. 'In the morning it will not be so hot, and I would not keep you long away.'

It was tempting. Matthew had curtly informed her that she could have the morning to herself since there was no further meeting until late afternoon. She'd been angry at his dismissive tone, and despondent that the small luxury of being close to him, even in the barren splendour of the opulent boardroom, was to be curtailed, and had wondered heavily how she would fill in the long hours without him. Now, the handsome doctor was providing her with a solution. She could immerse herself in the experience he offered and satisfy her natural curiosity about this very different culture.

Impulsively, she nodded. 'You've twisted my arm,' she capitulated, and laughed at the look of puzzled concern on his face. 'I mean, you've persuaded me. I'll come.'

His face cleared and he smiled delightedly. 'Thank you. I will come for you at ten o'clock tomorrow, if that's convenient.'

'Yes. That will be fine.'

Tony Amhurst passed by on his way through the gardens and looked in her direction. Thea bit her lip as the doctor chose that very moment to seize her hand and carry it exuberantly to his lips.

Tony paused, as though he was about to come over and intervene. Thea hurriedly retrieved her hand and waved it airily, and he continued, with obvious reluctance, on his way.

He mentioned the incident to her at dinner.

'I don't think you should be too chummy with the locals, my dear. They're a hot-blooded lot and their customs are not ours, you know.'

Thea set her chin. 'I'm not encouraging him, and I don't think I can come to much harm visiting the hospital with him.'

Tony started, his large mouth dropping open in horror.

'You're not actually going to go out with the fellow? Matthew will have a fit.'

'My visit to the hospital can hardly be classed as

"going out",' she said, her breast heaving with
sudden fury as she thought of the way Matthew had
ignored her, while placing her coldly and deliberately
in the hands of a gaoler. She was his paid-for property
until such time as he chose to dispense with her. A
vision arose of Muriel's tense, white face as she'd sat
in the outer office awaiting his pronouncement of her
fate, and Thea wondered if her own fate would be as
cruel. She shook with barely controlled anger.

'You may tell Mr Clayburn from me that I won't
allow him to dictate to me about where and with
whom I should spend my morning off. All that needs
to concern him with regard to me is that I turn up in
time for the meeting, and I will undertake to do that.
Nothing more.'

A foolhardy challenge, and she'd half expected
Matthew to seek her out in explosive wrath; she didn't
know whether to be relieved or disappointed when he
didn't.

In the event, she spent a restless night and dreamed
of the doctor, still handsome but somehow sinister in
flowing native robes, sweeping her up on to his white
horse. Even as she slept, she knew it was ridiculous.
White horses came from Arabia.

As they galloped away into the desert, she saw
Matthew's face ravaged by the despair of losing her,
and wanted desperately to go back to comfort him.

The doctor called promptly at ten o'clock to pick
her up in a gleamingly expensive German car, and
Thea's eyes widened.

He saw her expression and laughed. 'Did you think
I was poor?'

Thea colourerd. 'I hadn't really thought about it.'

He seemed pleased at her momentary awe. 'I am
rich enough to take four wives,' he assured her as they

drove smoothly along the dry, sandy coast road.

Thea swallowed her breath and spluttered, covering her embarrassment with a cough and a wave of the hand which indicated the dust rising from the road.

He wasn't fooled. 'I surprise you. Did you not know our religion permits four wives?'

Thea shook her head. 'No,' she replied, still breathless. 'Isn't that a bit excessive?'

He laughed. 'The more wives a man has, the more children he will be borne. Ten . . . twenty . . . perhaps more.'

She nodded faintly. 'I can see how you would need to be rich.'

'Oh, yes. Because four wives will bring four—how must I say it—mothers-in-law who will probably live longer than their husbands, and I must take them in. I must provide also for my own mother and my unmarried sisters.'

'Good heavens!' Thea said, overwhelmed with the thought of a house bursting at the seams with women. 'How many wives have you got at the moment?'

He smiled, teeth dazzlingly white against his brown skin.

'None. I have been too busy with my studies. His eyes shone at her. 'Perhaps I will choose only one wife, if she fulfils me.'

Thea laughed. 'You could hardly expect the poor woman to bear you twenty children.'

He shrugged. 'Perhaps not. But she might bring other compensations.'

His eyes darkened intensely, and Thea moved uncomfortably. She could smell the faint, exotic perfume of him, and was suddenly short of air.

'Is the hosiptal much further away?' she asked, changing the subject abruptly. To her relief he turned his attention to the road and slowed the car at the next road, which was narrower, but tarmacked smooth.

'We are already here,' he said, and Thea sighed gratefully.

Her tour of the hospital, small by some standards and far from well equipped, was interesting but a little disturbing. She was glad when the doctor indicated their visit was over.

'We have a small dining-room for staff, and I should be happy to give you some refreshment.'

Thea stole a glance at her watch. It was coming up to noon, and the meeting would begin at three o'clock.

'I don't know if I have time.'

He looked disappointed and put a hand lightly on her arm. 'Please. Accept my hospitality.'

Thea capitulated, and then had a frightening picture of herself trying to force down a sheep's eye delicacy.

'A . . . a cup of coffee is all I could manage,' she said shakily.

He smiled and nodded. 'My pleasure.'

The dining-room was rather better furnished than the wards, its wall mosaicked, its tables and seats low and similarly mosaicked in brilliant colours.

Thea's pleasure in its beauty was spoiled immediately she stepped in and met the icy blue glare directed at her across the room. Her heart stopped and then thudded into loud and uneven life again.

What on earth was Matthew Clayburn doing here? she asked herself dazedly, and then answered with the obvious. Tony Amhurst had delivered her message and he was here to wreak vengenace.

He lifted an imperious hand to her, indicating she could come to him, and she seethed as she obeyed, aware of a number of pairs of dark eyes following her progress. The young doctor looked faintly sullen with disappointment, but shook hands politely with the unexpected visitor.

'Won't you introduce me?' Matthew said cordially, as chips of blue ice bored into Thea's resentful violet eyes.

She coloured and began stonily, 'Mr Matthew Clayburn, may I present Dr . . .'

Thea, struggling to keep her anger under control racked her brain for a name, but found none.

The doctor stepped forward politely, his eyes almost as cold as Matthew's, and half hooded now by heavy, dark-fringed lids.

'I am Hassan.' He offered his hand stiffly for Matthew to shake. Their hands touched briefly before he stood back and took Thea lightly by the elbow.

'Please now be seated and I will order your coffee.'

He indicated a table some way from his obviously unwelcome visitor, and she started to move towards it.

Matthew stood suddenly, startling the man beside him.

'I'm afraid we haven't time,' he said somewhat brusquely. 'Miss Lawson and I have an important meeting to attend quite shortly. Perhaps we can repay your hospitality some other time.'

Narrowed brown met steel-hardened blue forcefully, and Thea stepped hastily between the men. The situation was getting rapidly out of hand.

'I'm afraid Mr Clayburn is right,' she said, smiling with all the charm she could muster at Hassan. 'I hope you won't be offended if we rush off.'

The doctor's expression softened a little, and he smiled with a return of warmth.

'I must not keep you from something of importance.' He took her hand and kissed it, his lips lingering against her fingers in a way that had Matthew's jaw clenching fiercely. Over the bent dark head, Thea flashed him a pleading glance, and he made a small impatient sound.

Thea's hand was returned to her lingeringly, and an intimate smile had her pulses jumping nervously. Thea wasn't sure if it was genuine warmth or deliberately goading, and if Matthew should lose his temper . . .

'We shall meet again,' the doctor said positively.

Thea looked anxiously at Matthew's flushed face, but sighed with relief as he turned away to take a polite farewell of his own hosts.

Driving back to the hotel, the atmosphere in the air-conditioned car was electric with tension.

Thea sat anxiously beside Matthew, alternating between the urge to apologise and a stormy desire to do battle.

Matthew broke the silence at last.

'I want it clearly understood that, in future, you will accept no invitation without my express permission. We are here to do a job of work, and I don't intend to waste precious time searching for a foolish woman who hasn't the faintest idea of the risks involved in making casual acquaintance here.'

White-hot anger washed away caution.

'Heavens above! The man's a doctor, not a white slaver or whatever other lurid occupation you're dreaming up for him. He was taking me on an ordinary tour of his hospital. Perfectly proper and perfectly safe. And there was absolutely no reason for you to come spying on me.'

'Don't be ridiculous!' he said bitingly. 'As it happened, and by sheer coincidence, I also was offered a tour. When Amhurst told me what you intended, I could have put a stop to it right away, but I knew I'd be there on the spot and decided to wait and see if common sense would prevail. I didn't take you for a fool.' His mouth twisted. 'It seems my confidence was misplaced.'

It hurt. Yes, it hurt like mad to meet the shaft of ridicule he sent her . . . the pain tightening in her chest until she could hardly breathe.

She didn't want to continue this argument. An urgent need arose to ask him why he had abandoned her, pushed her out in the cold to freeze to death in the deadening heat of Morocco. And to tell him that, if only he would ask with love, she would follow him to the ends of the earth, muffled up in concealing robes like the Moroccan women if that was what he wanted, her eyes averted from every man but him.

CHAPTER SEVEN

THE LOUNGE was full of people, mostly holiday makers, but with some Moroccans here and there, to see the snake charmer. Thea sat alone, having told Tony Amhurst very pointedly to go away. He went, and Thea sighed with relief.

Her thoughts were turned inwards and she gave up all pretence of reading the novel she was holding, engrossing herself instead in her misery.

Since her visit to the hospital yesterday, Tony Amhurst had barely left her side.

'I feel as though you're stuck to me with glue,' she'd said resentfully. 'Has the lord and master insisted on a tightening of security?'

He'd grinned, quite unoffended. 'Something like that.' He'd squeezed her arm in a friendly gesture. 'Never mind. Three more days and we'll be home. You can do as you like then.'

Thea had looked at him, her stomach churning. He'd sounded so positive. Had Matthew discussed his plans with Tony? Was this his way of preparing her for dismissal? She wished she dared ask Tony outright, but knew she wouldn't be able to stand the humiliation of having her worst fears confirmed by anyone other than Matthew.

People were moving the furniture about, making space for the snake charmer, and Thea was startled to find herself surrounded on all sides by a rather boisterous crowd, all wearing smiles of eager anticipation. In the middle of all the hilarity and anticipation, she felt more miserable than ever, and would have got up to leave if she could have found space to move.

As her eyes swept the room, seeking an avenue of escape, they met the warm brown gaze of Hassan. He waved, indicating he would come to her as soon as the crowd dispersed, and her heart sank. She hadn't seen him since yesterday, and had half hoped he would have got the message and stayed away. She really had nothing to say to him, and his presence here would only cause added complications.

Looking away from him, her gaze was caught again, this time in a sea of cornflower-blue venom. The lowering dark bridge of eyebrows across a powerful nose left her in no doubt that there was trouble ahead. Tearing her eyes away, she wondered, with a little shiver, if Matthew had seen the exchange between herself and Hassan.

A feeling of helplessness was followed by anger. Let them fight it out between themselves, she thought rebelliously. She would remain an interested bystander.

But she was deluding herself. She knew she would never be allowed to opt out of the power battle.

She turned her attention deliberately to the performance of the snake charmer, who was writhing about on the floor in apparent agony, having put half a dozen snakes down his voluminous trousers, but some sixth sense prickled along the back of her neck, telling her that Matthew was getting nearer. Her stomach clenched with apprehension, her nerves stretching with tension. They reached breaking-point seconds later when a snake came unexpectedly flying through the air to coil about her throat.

She screamed in panic and jumped from her seat,

overturning a small table and its contents of drinks, dragging the thing from her neck with a hand that shook with terror. It took a few seconds for her to realise that she was holding, not a snake, but a supple leather belt.

The noise ceased momentarily, as her scream hung in the air and people stared at her. The tense silence was followed almost immediately by laughter as everyone realised the 'joke'.

Thea burst into tears, her humiliation complete as she found herself unable to move from the spot, hemmed in by chairs and people, her body shaking with reaction and shame. How could she have screamed like that at a harmless belt? She lowered her head and covered her face with her hands.

A hard grip caught her wrists, dragging them down, and she was staring into Matthew's granite face. Before she could register her surprise, he'd lifted her bodily into his arms and was clearing the way with aggressive thrusts of his shoulders.

Thea's mortification increased. Instead of feeling grateful, she felt an overpowering urge to murder. Her hands, holding on about his neck, flexed with a desire to strangle him. None of this would have happened if he had only been able to treat her with moderate friendliness, instead of with steely disdain which left her wondering brokenly what she had done to deserve his painful rejection. Trying to deny her feelings, thrusting them down, had wound her up tighter than a drum. It had taken a stupid joke to trigger off the explosion.

Her body trembled against his and she thought he drew her closer. The small movement sent heat rushing through her chilled body, draining her strength, leaving her limp and clinging in his arms.

It wasn't until they were out in the blessed darkness of the gardens that he finally put her on her feet.

'Can you stand?'

His hands, holding her securely by the waist, made it harder rather than easier to steady herself, but somehow she managed it.

'Yes, I think so.'

'I ought to go back in there and wring that idiot's neck,' he growled fiercely. 'What made him think that stupid trick was funny?'

Thea was still shaking from shock and the automatic reaction of her body close to his. She had meant to thank him for his help and concern, but instead found herself attacking him.

'I'm sorry I made a fool of myself. But don't worry, it won't rub off on you. We've been together so little in public since we got here, I don't think people will make the connection.'

Her voice was so bitter, so harsh, that he stared at her in surprise. He took his hands away suddenly, leaving her rocking on her feet.

'Have you known me this long without realising that I don't give a damn for what *people* think?'

Thea took a shuddering breath. 'No, I can't say I haven't noticed that.' She bit her lip to stop the sudden, senseless tears.

He nodded his satisfaction at her answer. 'Then why the nonsense?'

She stared up at him, hoping for some sign that he cared what *she* felt about him, but there was none.

'Perhaps because I wanted to hurt you,' she said at last. 'Just as you've been hurting me ever since we came here. I'd like to be cold and hateful just like you, and make you feel you don't exist.'

For a moment he was still, his eyes dark, unreadable

pools, and then he seemed to shrug himself together.

'You don't know what you're saying.' He gripped her shoulders with hands that hurt. 'I don't know whether to give you a glass of brandy or a good shaking.'

Thea's lip trembled. She'd told him the truth, bared her soul, hoping for tenderness, understanding. Instead, he was brushing off what she said as the ramblings of a shocked schoolgirl.

Tears gathered on the rims of her eyes, halted there by the surge of frustrated fury.

'Is that all you can say?'

The pressure of his hands on her arms slackened, and the hard radiance of his eyes softened momentarily, filling her with a flare of hope.

'Thea, I've already made enough of a mess of these negotiations. I brought you here as my secretary to help me, not as a constant source of anxiety and irritation, drawing my attention from important issues.' He shook her, his face awash with exasperation. 'This isn't the time for anything else, Thea.'

'I'm sorry,' Thea said, her voice thick with mortification. 'I didn't realise how much trouble I was causing you. As it happens, you could have saved yourself the anxiety of spying on me. You can call off your tame watchdog. I'm quite capable of taking care of myself. I've been doing it for long enough.'

Matthew's jaw tightened and he pulled her roughly towards him. 'You little fool! You've just no idea, have you . . . of the way men think? No idea of the way you look . . . or what those big innocent eyes do to a . . .' He stopped, an angry growl taking the place of words. 'When we get home, things are going to have to be sorted out. I can't let it go on like this . . .'

Thea stiffened in his grasp, waiting for him to say it. Waiting for him to tell how yet another secretary had let him down by falling in love. She had told him, confirmed his worst suspicions, and now there was no hope.

'If you're thinking of sacking me,' she said with a brave toss of her head, 'I'll save you the trouble by tendering my resignation. You'll have it in writing in the morning.'

She had no idea how she would bring herself to do it and then struggle through the hell of the next three days.

An expression that could almost have been anguish crossed his face, but as it contorted into a fierce scowl she knew she'd been wrong. He was just furious.

He released her with a little push, that felt as though he was pushing her out of his life, releasing himself from any lingering sense of commitment.

'OK. If that's the way you want it.'

Their eyes locked, Thea's probing his for something she knew in her heart didn't exist.

'Yes,' she said, her voice low and shaky. 'That's the way I want it.'

She turned from him. At least, when there was nothing else to save, she could save her pride.

Half blinded by tears, she had difficulty focusing on the dark man coming towards her, a white smile lighting his face.

When she recognised him, her heart sank even more heavily.

'Thea!'

Two male voices spoke almost in unison, each demanding her urgent attention.

With a cry half of despair, half of fury, she turned from them both and ran up the steps towards the hotel, reaching the tall, brown-tinted, sliding window at almost the same time as a man on the other side.

He collided with the window as though he had no idea it was there, and Thea wondered briefly if he was drunk. In the next second the whole window splintered and cascaded, in seeming slow motion, down at Thea's feet. After a split second's delay she jumped back into the strong arms that lifted her away. Through her own shock, she felt the trembling of the body that held her.

She was turned around and held against a tensely hard chest in which the heart thundered like a maddened bird. She looked up into Matthew's chalk-white face.

'My God, Thea! You could have been killed!'

Her whole body shuddering, she buried her face in the hollow of his neck.

'Oh, Matthew!' It was an agonised cry of need, and he gathered her closer still, crushing her to him as though he would never let her go, and she was more than happy to stay there in his arms.

'Thea! Miss Lawson! Are you all right?'

The attractively accented voice broke between them, and Thea lifted her head to look into Hassan's troubled gaze.

Matthew's body grew even more rigid and his eyes were brittle with rage.

'Thank you for your enquiry, Mr Hassan,' he said with tight civility. 'But Miss Lawson is perfectly safe with me. I don't think you need to concern yourself further.'

Ignoring the probing stare directed at him, Hassan kept his eyes on Thea, taking in the white face which had now begun to burn with two bright spots of colour.

'You are in shock. Please let me help you. Have you been cut?'

Thea shook her head. 'I don't think so. I . . . I was lucky.'

'I don't think you realise how lucky. If the glass had flown outwards, instead of collapsing downwards the way it did, you'd have been cut to shreds.'

Thea shuddered and felt an answering tremor in Matthew.

'I don't think we need any more graphic descriptions, Hassan.' Matthew's voice was cold. 'And since you are a doctor, I suppose it might be as well if you took a look at Miss Lawson to make sure she's escaped injury.' He frowned heavily at the Moroccan. 'In my presence, of course.'

'But of course.'

Hassan smiled, but his brown eyes narrowed over a jutting nose that suddenly looked every bit as ruthless as Matthew's and held the icy-blue stare with an ease and assurance that had Thea trembling visibly. They looked like two bristling dogs about to start a fight.

'If you don't mind,' she said shakily, 'I think I'd like to lie down.'

Hassan looked apologetic. Matthew looked annoyed.

'Then what are we waiting for?' he said brusquely, and made as though to lift her up in his arms.

Thea resisted. 'If you don't mind, I think I've been carried around enough for one day.'

With reluctance, Matthew took her arm and glared murderously at Hassan who was taking her other arm.

Their attitude both infuriated and unnerved her, but she was too weak to be anything but grateful for their support.

Someone had recruited a British nurse who was on

holiday in the hotel, and she followed them up to Thea's room to help her into her nightdress and to act as chaperon during the examination. Matthew was banished to the far corner of her room, where he stood, staring moodily out of her window, until the doctor had satisfied himself there were no injuries.

'I still can't believe the miracle of your escape,' he said with a shake of his head.

'Thea has nine lives.' Matthew had crossed the room and was standing beside the bed, looking down at her with a mixture of relief and exasperation showing on his face. 'At the moment, she's using them up at a rate of knots, and it's playing havoc with my nervous system.'

Thea coloured hotly

Hassan looked uncomprehending.

'It's a long story,' Matthew said with a small quirk of his lips, 'and one I find too harrowing to repeat at the moment.' He held out his hand to the doctor. 'Thank you for your help. You'll let me have your bill, of course.'

Hassan flinched as though Matthew had struck him, and dark brows lowered over his heavy-lidded eyes.

'That is kind of you, Mr Clayburn. But I don't accept payment for tending a friend.' He turned from Matthew and took Thea's hand, lifting it to his lips. 'I've given you a mild sedative. Sleep now and I will see you later.'

Thea caught Matthew's furious scowl over Hassan's bent head, and correctly read the words on his lips. This, she thought unhappily, was the worst day of her life. It was obvious he hated all the trouble she was causing him, and she wished it was possible to go home and feel her pain and misery in peace.

Perhaps, since she'd given him her resignation, he might be willing to find her an earlier flight back and let her go.

Her head felt woozy already from the sedative Hassan had given her, but she hardly dared let her eyes close for fear of what might happen between Matthew and Hassan. Their aggression filled the room with disturbing electricity.

'I think you gentlemen had better settle the question of finances outside,' the pert, dark-haired nurse cut in heavily. 'The patient can hardly keep her eyes open. She needs to rest.'

It was heaven to have some support from any quarter, and Thea closed her eyes with a sigh. As she began to sink into sleep, she thought the nurse was quite capable of sorting both men out if necessary.

'Are you awake? I've brought you something to drink.'

Thea's lids fluttered open.

'You've been asleep for a couple of hours. I thought it was time I woke you. Are you feeling better?'

The nurse was smiling down at her and Thea struggled groggily to sit up.

'How . . . how long have you been here?'

'For quite a while. I thought I'd better stand guard. I didn't trust either of your admirers not to come sneaking back here the minute my back was turned.'

Thea groaned. 'They're not my admirers. One's my boss and interested only in getting the job done, and the other's a local doctor who took me on a tour of the hospital. I hardly know him.'

The dark eyes widened in amusement. 'You mean they're both up for grabs? This is my lucky day.'

Thea laughed sourly. 'Best of luck. You'll need it

with both of them.'

Strange, she mused, how the same day could mean such opposite things to two people.

A knock sounded on the door.

'Which one is it?' the nurse said, softly conspiratorial. 'My money's on the boss.'

Thea gave a resigned nod of her head. 'I don't think you'll lose it. He's probably brought my notebook with him.'

'I wouldn't want to bet on *that*.' The nurse shot a wryly amused look over her shoulder as she went to open the door. 'When he left here, I swear the last thing he had on his mind was work.'

Perhaps you're right, Thea thought cynically. He was probably thinking of murdering Hassan. He wasn't used to being stood up to.

But it was Hassan who followed the nurse into the room, and Thea didn't know whether to be relieved or disappointed. In any event, she felt uneasy. The words she'd read on Matthew's lips when Hassan had promised to call back to see her had been 'over my dead body'.

She shivered with apprehension. At the moment she was in no condition to cope with his anger, nor with Dr Hassan's solicitude. He sat on the corner of Thea's bed and seemed about to make himself at home.

'I'm fine . . . fine,' she said hastily in answer to his query. 'It was only nerves. The rest has done me good. In fact, I was just about to get up.'

The doctor looked shocked. 'But it is almost ten o'clock. I was about to give you another sedative to help you sleep the night.'

'Oh, no,' Thea said. 'I really must get up to stretch my legs before I settle down again.'

She looked beseechingly at the nurse.

'Yes. I think that's a good idea. As soon as you leave, I'll help the patient into a nice, relaxing bath. It's just what she needs. Don't you agree, Doctor?'

Hassan stood up with the assistance of the nurse's hand beneath his elbow. He seemed a little nervous as the dark eyes smiled into his.

He looked almost bewildered as he stole a last look at Thea.

She hid a smile. The girl's technique was wonderful, and probably a necessity for survival on wards full of male doctors.

'By the way,' Thea heard her say as she shepherded Hassan to the door, 'I'd be so interested to look over your local hospital. Would it be possible for you to arrange if for me?'

And that, thought Thea in relief, is the last I'll see of Dr Hassan . . . I hope.

CHAPTER EIGHT

'THEA! Wake up!'

Thea was floating on a warm sea, her head as light as a cloud somehow detached from her body. A deep voice penetrated her bliss.

'You little fool. Wake up!'

With a sense of intrusion, she pulled herself irritably from her peaceful place and opened her eyes.

Cornflower-blue eyes met hers angrily. 'You might have drowned.'

He was kneeling beside the sunken bath, glaring down at her.

'I . . . I wasn't asleep,' she defended, weak but defiant. 'I was just resting . . . trying to get a bit of peace.'

He grunted. 'You'd have found it, perfect and permanent, if I hadn't come in.'

'Don't exaggerate,' Thea argued, but she was shaking inside.

Perhaps it had been foolish to refuse the nurse's offer of help and send her away, but she'd been desperate for a little solitude to try to sort out the riot of her feelings. Sleep had seemed the farthest thing from her at the time, but obviously she hadn't reckoned on the lingering effects of the sedative.

'I'm getting rather tired of your implications that I invite accidents.'

Thea glared at him, only to find that his attention had wandered, his eyes moving slowly over her body, which was barely concealed by the scented foam.

Her colour flared immediately, and she made a foolish

gesture of concealment.

He grinned slowly. 'Spoilsport.'

'If you can take time off from your observations to hand me a towel,' Thea said icily, 'I'd like to get out.'

His grin widened. 'And if I don't . . . what will you do?'

Thea squirmed. It was bad enough to have him here, looking her over lazily as though she was a prize exhibit, but far worse to know there wasn't a thing she could do about it, except stand up and run. Perhaps that was what he was waiting for. She sank deeper into the water and closed her eyes. 'Stay here until I freeze to death, I suppose.'

'Stubborn, hopeless little fool,' he murmured softly.

A hand touched her forehead, lightly traced the outline of her nose and lips and descended to the side of her throat. Thea remained rigid, not daring to open her eyes for fear of letting him see the excitement that had begun treacherously to burn through her.

'Get out,' she whispered in hoarse fury.

He took his hand away and stood up.

Thea stayed rigidly still, waiting for the sound of the door closing behind him, but it didn't come. In the next instant, a hand had grasped her wrists and pulled her firmly upright, startled and exposed. Her eyes flew open in outrage.

Before she could protest, a large, soft towel was thrown about her and she was lifted bodily from the bath, her arms imprisoned, her wet hair lying against his shoulder.

'Matthew!' she wailed. 'What on earth do you think you're doing?'

He carried her out of the bathroom, down the two steps into the living-room and across to the large armchair close to the elaborately arched window.

'What I should have done right from the start . . . talk some sense into you.'

Thea stifled an hysterical giggle. Talk was all he had in mind . . . when her pulse was jumping madly and her skin was afire with the feel of his body against hers through the damp towel. The dampness had already penetrated his shirt, and she felt the warmth of him as though there was nothing in between.

'Matthew, I don't think this is the right moment. That nurse might be coming back at any minute. She promised to tuck me in.'

'Damn!' he cursed. 'Or more likely that damned doctor.'

With a sudden movement he put Thea from him, leaving her cold and strangely lonely outside his arms. 'You're a magnet for medics,' he said grimly. 'And while I can understand it, I don't intend to encourage it.'

He moved purposefully towards the door, and Thea's heart began bumping nervously. He was going to find Hassan. She hugged the towel about herself, feeling helpless. She was in no condition to withstand another confrontation between the two men.

But he didn't open the door. Instead, she heard a click and realised with surprise and a quick start of shock that he'd turned the lock.

'There,' he said with satisfaction. 'Now we should have some peace.'

He was coming purposefully towards her, and Thea felt a rising surge of panic. 'Can't this wait until tomorrow?'

'No. It's got to be tonight.'

'Then at least give me time to get dressed.'

Matthew gripped her arms and, sitting down in the armchair, drew her firmly on to his lap, hooking his arm comfortably about her waist.

'I like you just the way you are.'

Thea felt light-headed with excitement that she was reluctant to quell. It felt good to be in his arms, helpless against him. If he was to kiss her now, she would be powerless to stop him.

She was startled to feel him pulling the towel from her shoulders, sliding the soft material from her arms, revealing the swell of her breasts and the raggedness of her breath.

'Matthew,' she pleaded. 'Don't.'

'Am I getting to you at last, Thea?' His voice was soft, warm with mischief. The gentle warmth of breath touched her cheek.

Her teeth bit into the soft flesh of her lower lip, which had begun to tremble, and she muttered a silent prayer for strength to stem the tide of feelings which threatened to engulf her.

'I'd rather you just said what you want to say.'

Was it relief or disappointment she felt as he pulled the towel up a little to cover her?

'Just don't wriggle about, Thea. I'm not made of stone.'

Thea hid a gasp and shot him a wide, questioning glance. But he was frowning now, a tight line deepening between nose and granite chin.

'You cheated me, Thea,' he said suddenly.

Thea tensed herself against the unexpected harshness of his voice and waited for him to go on. So, it had come to the crunch. She wished desperately that he had allowed her to get dressed. She felt devoid of defences, completely vulnerable here in his arms, naked and feeling the strong beat of his heart against her own.

'All I wanted was a secretary. Someone who'd give me no hassle. Someone who'd just be content to get the job done . . . do as she was told . . . and leave me in peace to get on with my work. I should have known better.'

'You're not being fair . . .' she began, stung by the censure in his tone. She wanted to tell him that was what she had wanted, too. Just to earn her money and go home, at peace with the world, to Aunt Edith and Leon. 'After all, it was you who chose me as suitable.'

It wasn't her fault it hadn't worked out that way. His magnetism had cut through the circuit to her common sense . . . cutting her adrift. She hadn't wanted to fall in love. The agony of that was the last thing in the world she wanted.

'Yes. I vetted the applications and made up the short list myself,' he agreed. 'They were all there . . . the closest thing to a bunch of nuns or ninety-year-olds. I couldn't go wrong. Then your application turned up. A day late, and by all the rules it should have been turned down.'

Thea's toes curled with embarrassment. Did he think she had tried to wangle her way in?

'I didn't know it was late,' she responded woodenly. 'If I had known I'd overshot the last date of application . . .'

'It wouldn't have made the smallest difference.'

Thea gave him a puzzled stare. 'Why not? Rules are rules.'

He laughed shortly. 'I make the rules. I bend them when I want to.'

'But why should you want to?' Thea was puzzled. His nearness was almost forgotten, the tingling excitement of his hand clasping her waist fading as her curiosity grew.

He smiled cynically. 'I saw you in the corridor about a week before and asked your name. When I saw that same name on your application form, I had a terrible sense of destiny.' He laughed with gentle self-mockery.

'I knew it was going to be you.'

'But . . . it didn't have to be. I didn't force you,' Thea argued. 'It was you who persuaded me. Remember?'

He snorted, and his finger reached up to toy with the sensitive lobe of her ear, his hand tightening about her waist as she shuddered in response.

'I don't believe in fighting destiny.'

Angry with herself for letting him see the effect he had on her, her fury spilled over. Galled by the unfairness of her situation, she lost her temper.

'Why did you bother? Why couldn't you have left me with Tom Griffiths, where I was happy?'

His eyes changed—grew brilliant with a hard light. 'Were you happier with Tom Griffiths than with me?'

Thea fought to be fair, despite his goading of her. 'I think perhaps I was. At least I knew where I was with Tom. He liked me and he trusted me.'

She sighed, remembering the halcyon days of peaceful co-existence she had so thoughtlessly given up to meet a hopeless challenge. 'I don't suppose you'd be agreeable to my going back to work for him now that I've given you my resignation. I really do need the job. The money isn't so good, but I'll learn all over again to get by.'

She looked at him hopefully, but he was shaking his head.

'Impossible.'

Tears began pricking the back of her eyes, but she defied them to fall. How could he be holding her so gently and yet be so cold, unfeeling, callous?

'But why? I'm a good secretary, with an excellent reputation for efficiency and getting on with my boss . . . until I started working for you.' She set her chin stubbornly. 'Surely you can't call a few mislaid files and one or two minor accidents good enough reason for dispensing with my services.'

'I don't have to give you reasons. You offered your resignation; I didn't ask for it, but I'm accepting it.'

A sob rose and pushed its way past her lips.

It was too late to care what he thought now, and she allowed the tears to fall unhindered.

'And you won't let me go back to Tom Griffiths?'

He shook his head slowly. 'No.'

'Damn you, Matthew Clayburn!' Thea's voice, cracked and broken, cursed him aloud.

With a wrenching motion, she tried to extricate herself from his arms, but he held her firmly.

'Let me go,' she sobbed harshly.

The towel lost its battle to provide cover and twisted around her body, exposing her firm breasts, but Thea was past caring, concerned only for her freedom.

'Not until you've heard what I have to say.'

Thea was enraged by the note of wry amusement in his voice and turned blazing eyes on him, only to be caught in a soft ocean of blue, which threatened to drown her in the most wonderful sensations.

'What's the point?' Thea's voice was almost inaudible. Mesmerised by his gaze, her resistance was already being washed away in cornflower seas.

'That's what I've been asking myself . . . over and over. You've been nothing but aggravation to me from day one, taking over my mind to the exclusion of everything else. Every day I promised myself it would be the last time you'd get under my skin.' He frowned irritably. 'The day I saw you with the baby was the worst. I thought you were married. Even when you assured me you weren't, I felt let down that you'd lied to me about Leon.'

Thea coloured. 'I didn't lie. Leon wasn't mine, so I didn't classify him exactly as a tie. Melissa was bound to take him back sooner or later.'

'And that was another blow. You see, I was already working out the pros and cons of having a ready-made family . . . and realising how much I liked the idea.'

Thea's heart began to pound uncomfortably. 'Matthew, what are you saying? I don't understand.'

'Don't you?' His eyes gleamed brightly. 'Do you mean you didn't know I was in love with you?'

Open-mouthed with shock, Thea stared at him. 'No. How could I? Most of the time you were horrible to me . . . dictatorial, overbearing, unreasonable. Is that your way of demonstrating love?'

He smiled, and his hand touched her breast almost idly.

'No, my sweet. It was my way of fighting it. But I can't go on fighting for much longer.'

Thea closed her eyes, unable to bear the agony of his touch. Her mind seemed to be on some kind of automatic pilot, hearing, interpreting, but not comprehending. Had he really said he loved her?

'Open your eyes, Thea. This is no time to hide.'

Matthew's thumb was creating giddying electric currents that were unbearable against her sensitive skin. She could feel the movement of his breath against her cheek and had an awful suspicion that his mouth was close to hers. Slowly warily, she opened her eyes.

His faced loomed close, his lips, as she'd suspected, a breath away.

'Marry me, Thea,' he murmured. 'It's the only way I'll manage to keep my sanity and go on running the Trust.'

Thea's eyes flew open and her fingers clung to his hand to stop the maddening movement.

'Marry you? Are . . . are you serious?'

His eyes narrowed intently, sending strange shivers up her spine. 'Never more serious.'

His head dipped and his lips slid along the curve of her throat. The shivers grew until her whole body shook.

'I . . . I don't know what to say.'

His mouth brushed her cheek, spreading fire to distract her. 'Just say yes. I want to kiss you.'

'Matthew, please! Don't tease. If you're serious, you have to give me time to think.'

'Yes, of course.' He kissed the tip of her nose. 'Take all the time you want. I can wait . . . as long as it's no more than five seconds.'

His hands caressed her waist, the supple curve of her back.

'One . . . two . . . three . . .' He counted. 'It's now or never, Thea. Yes or no.

Thea's breath caught in her throat. 'Yes. All right, yes. I'll marry you.'

'Good,' he murmured softly. His lips curved sensuously. 'Now, where was I?'

Thea couldn't answer, because his mouth covered hers and the world disappeared. She might have been in heaven or outer space and she wouldn't have noticed or cared. The centre of her being was here in his arms, revolving around the sensation of loving and being loved . . . feeling his hands in her hair, his lips against her brow, her eyes, her mouth, the arching curve of her throat.

'Thea,' he murmured her name, setting her aflame. 'My sweet, sweet Thea.'

'Oh, Matthew,' she sighed. 'I love you.'

His hold on her tightened. 'I thought you'd never say it.'

Possessively, he pulled her to him, growling with frustration at the material barrier between them. 'Let's get rid of this damned towel.'

CHAPTER NINE

'BUT, Matthew, surely you're not going to insist on my resignation now?'

'I most certainly am.'

For two whole days, Thea had been floating above the clouds with happiness. Now, sitting beside Matthew as they flew ten thousand feet above the earth, she came down with a bump.

'Please, don't be unreasonable. I like my job. I don't want to give it up.'

He sighed, a small sound of exasperation, and took her hand.

'It's you who's being unreasonable. Once we're married you won't need a job. I'll take care of you and your aunt, and little Leon, if necessary. You'll have more than enough to do with your energy.'

The reassuring pressure of his fingers filled her with warmth and she returned it, but with a continuing sense of uneasiness.

'We won't all fit into your flat, Matthew,' she insisted. 'And with a housekeeper on the premises there would hardly be enough housework to keep us both occupied.'

Matthew looked thoughtful. 'Don't worry about Pearson,' he said. 'I may dispense with his services as my housekeeper. I've something else in mind for him. He's jack of all trades and a very efficient master of most of them.'

Thea bit her lip. The word 'efficient' cut through her like a knife. Was it her seeming inefficiency which was behind his insistence on holding her to her resignation?

If it was, then he wasn't being fair. She'd had very little time to show him how good she could be, and everything stacked against her.

'Perhaps you should make him your next secretary,' she said tartly. 'At least if I'm being forced to stay at home, I shan't have to worry about your new secretary falling in love with you.'

His head swivelled round, his eyes lit with amused incredulity. 'Ah!' he said in the manner of one who had solved the mystery of the universe. 'So that's why you are so insistent on remaining. You want to keep an eye on me.' He shook his head sadly. 'Surely, Thea, love is a question of trust.'

Thea's face reddened. It was true, though she'd been trying to keep it from herself. The thought of another woman working that closely with Matthew, falling in love with him, as she inevitably would, was creating havoc with her peace of mind.

'I do trust you,' she said a little sheepishly. 'It's the secretary I'm worried about. After all, don't forget, I've experienced what working in close proximity with you does to a poor defenceless woman.'

He smiled wickedly, leaning close, so that she could feel his breath against her cheek.

'A revelation I'll no doubt find fascinating,' he murmured. 'Let's save it up for later.'

His lips brushed hers quickly and Thea looked disappointed.

'Matthew!' It seemed suddenly urgent that he kiss her properly.

He nodded understanding, but waved an expressive hand at their fellow passengers. 'We'll save that for later, too.'

Thea sighed with frustration, but had to be content with the warm tenderness of his hand holding hers for the rest of the flight.

Edith was thrilled with the news of Matthew's proposal.

'I just knew it!' she said, clasping her hands exultantly. 'You two are just made for one another.'

Thea laughed. 'If you mean we're two of a kind, I hope not. He's demanding, self-opinionated and incredibly determined.'

Edith gave her a sly look. 'And warm, delicious and incredibly sexy.'

Thea's mouth opened in mock surprise. 'Really, Aunt! What can you mean?'

Edith hugged her. 'If you don't know yet, you're going to have a wonderful time finding out.'

Thea actually blushed.

It had been wonderful. Two exquisite days of sensations she hadn't known existed. In his arms she'd found an ocean of tenderness . . . and the ecstatic peak of passion. The memories shivered through her nervous system.

She could hardly bear the wait until he came this evening.

He'd acceded to her determination to work out a month's notice, but insisted on dropping her off at home on his way to the office. Their parting kiss had been a disappointingly brief one as he'd leaned over to open the car door for her.

'I won't come in now,' he said quickly. 'See you tonight about seven-thirty. If you feel up to it, we could go out to dinner.'

'Mmm. Lovely,' Thea responded automatically, but her heart was thumping with disappointment. The last thing in the world she wanted was to be with him in public. If she could persuade her aunt to take an evening off, she might be able to have him all to herself.

'Or if you'd prefer it, I could always cook you a meal,' she suggested tentatively.

His smile teased her. 'Do you mean you can cook?'

'Of course!' Thea said indignantly. 'Though it probably won't be up to the impeccable standard of your chef. Or does Pearson do the cooking as well as everything else?'

'Certainly he does. And as you say, he's cordon bleu.'

Thea frowned. 'I think I could grow to hate Pearson.'

Matthew grinned. 'Don't worry about it. I'm sure whatever you do, it will be quite adequate.' He shot her a slyly mocking glance.

Thea glared. 'No more than adequate?'

Matthew laughed into her furious face and his hand cupped her cheek in a heart-melting gesture. 'And if I'm still hungry, I could always eat you,' he said softly. 'Have I told you lately you're delicious?'

'Not lately,' Thea murmured. 'Could you tell me again?'

She offered him her lips.

'Temptress.' He shook his head. 'But there's no time now. See you at seven-thirty.'

Edith had been more than anxious to be accommodating. She rang a friend and arranged to call around for a visit.

'Thea's entertaining her fiancé at home,' Thea heard her say on the telephone, and felt herself colour. But the pride and pleasure in her aunt's voice warmed her heart. 'She's marrying the most gorgeous man imaginable.'

And he *was* gorgeous, Thea reaffirmed as she went into the hall later to answer the doorbell. Well worth the expense of the large joint of beef, presently roasting to perfection in the oven.

It was five minutes to seven, and her heart skipped

with joy. He was early. Obviously as anxious as she for them to be together.

But it wasn't Matthew who met her dazzling smile of welcome with a cynical grin.

'I'm sure that effusion isn't for me.'

'Melissa!' Thea's smiled faded. 'This *is* a surprise.'

'It shouldn't be that much of a surprise,' Melissa said drily as she pushed past Thea into the hall. 'After all, it was you who asked me to come urgently.'

'I wouldn't call over a week urgent.' Thea's uneasiness made her bitter. 'And Leon's already been put to bed.' He'd gone up early, worn out by the excitement of Thea's return. She'd been touched by his obvious pleasure at seeing her, and was reluctant now to disturb him from his sleep to the added upheaval of his mother's presence. 'It might be better if you came again during the day.'

Melissa shot her an impatient glance over her shoulder as she entered the living-room.

'There's no pleasing you, is there, Thea? There never was.'

Thea felt the familiar churning sense of frustration Melissa inevitably aroused in her, but forbore to answer the obvious invitation to a quarrel.

Edith, obviously hearing voices, came in from the kitchen and stopped short in surprise at the sight of her younger niece.

'Melissa,' she said at last, 'how nice!'

Melissa's mouth curled in a cynical smile. 'A slightly better welcome than the one I've just had from my sister.' She crossed to her aunt and kissed her cheek. 'How's everything?'

Edith recovered quickly.

'Fine. And if you mean Leon, he's more than fine . . . blooming, in fact.'

Melissa hooked her arm about her aunt's shoulders, led her to the settee and drew her cosily down beside her.

'I've got an hour to spare before I have to be at the theatre, so why don't you tell me all about it?' She looked up at her sister. 'Thea doesn't seem so keen for me to see Leon now I'm here, but I'm sure she won't mind my hearing about him.'

Thea's lips tightened. 'I just didn't want to disturb him when he'd already gone to sleep,' she said defensively. 'But you're his mother . . . and if you don't mind upsetting him . . .'

Thea's glowing sense of anticipation had disappeared, and in its place was a gnawing anxiety. She'd had time to forget how disturbing an influence Melissa could be.

Thea had been twenty—the same age as Melissa was now—when her parents had died, leaving her to care for her young sister, then a rebellious fifteen-year-old. Between them, she and Edith had managed to control her excesses, to some degree, and to make allowances for the devastating effect of their parents' death. Thea had hoped her sister would come to terms with it and become less resentful as she grew older. But it hadn't happened. If anything, she'd become even more unruly and disruptive, and Thea was remembering now how much of a relief it had been when she'd finally left home.

Looking at her sister's challenging expression, it was obvious her current success had done little to alleviate her earlier resentments.

'Perhaps Melissa could peep in on Leon before she goes,' Edith said, pouring oil on to the obviously troubled waters. 'It's only natural she should want to see him.'

Somehow, this peace bid put Thea in the wrong, and she saw the flash of triumph in Melissa's eyes.

She nodded uneasily, her gaze moving unconsciously to the clock, which said almost seven-fifteen. Matthew would be here soon. She wished there was some way she could put him off, but he would already have left the office. For some reason, she was deeply reluctant to have him meet Melissa again, to risk the tarnishing effect of her sister's cynical spite against her precious happiness. It was foolish, she knew, because they would be bound to come together sooner or later.

'Are you expecting someone?' Melissa cut into her thoughts.

Thea flushed dully, wishing she could deny it, but knew it was pointless.

'Yes. Matthew will be here shortly . . . for dinner.'

'He and Thea are getting married,' Edith put in proudly. 'Isn't it wonderful?'

Thea saw the brief, surprised widening of Melissa's eyes before the heavily fringed lids lowered.

'Congratulations. I hope you'll be happy.'

'Thank you.'

Thea wished with all her heart that her sister's wish had been sincere.

'Oh, I'm sure they will be,' Edith enthused. 'He's such a lovely man.'

'Is he?'

Melissa's casual query seemed to hold a wealth of meaning, mercifully lost on Edith, but touching Thea's heart with an icy chill.

'Actually, I know Matthew Clayburn very well. As a matter of fact, rather better than Thea, I imagine.'

She smiled into Thea's guarded face.

'You never did explain how.' Thea sounded composed, but her heart was bumping unevenly, making her wonder if she really wanted to know.

'Didn't I?' Melissa paused. 'Well, I met him about two years ago. Or more precisely, a year and nine months ago . . . I have a particular reason for remembering so explicitly.' She smiled, relishing the suddenly rapt attention. 'He put up the money for a play I was in at the time, and I was introduced to him later.'

'And?' Thea prompted, knowing there was more to come, and feeling a strange premonition she wasn't going to like the rest of it. 'What happened?'

Melissa's smile was malicious. 'Perhaps you should ask Matthew.'

As though on cue, the doorbell rang.

Thea's feet dragged as she went out into the hall. She'd been longing all day for this moment, now she didn't even know if she could cope with it.

What on earth's the matter with you? she admonished herself. You should know better than to let Melissa get under your skin.

As soon as she opened the door, Matthew took her in his arms.

'God, Thea! The day's been an age long.'

To emphasise his words, his mouth covered hers hungrily. Thea clung to him as though she feared he'd be snatched out of her arms.

After a while, he drew back and looked down at her with a rueful smile.

'I can see you've missed me, too.' He slipped an arm about her waist as they moved towards the living-room. 'Later, you can show me again how much . . .'

'Are you hungry?' Thea said, with a desperate calmness.

'Ravenous.' He pulled her close and whispered against her ear. 'Ravenous . . . for you.'

She let him kiss her again, but her nervousness swept away her response.

He lifted his head and looked down at her in concern. 'What's the matter?'

She shook her head warningly and said in a low voice,

'Melissa's here.'

'Ah!' he said, with a peculiar grimness.

'I've just heard your good news!' Melissa said, giving Matthew a bright smile. 'Congratulations! Do I get a sisterly kiss?'

Matthew took her outstretched hand and kissed her briefly.

Melissa touched his cheek. 'Quite like old times,' she said fondly.

'Is it?' He moved away from her to stand beside Thea. 'I'm afraid I don't quite recall the *old* times.'

'Don't you?' Melissa's eyes glinted. 'Never mind. If you think hard enough. I'm sure you will.'

Edith came in from the kitchen.

'Matthew! How lovely to see you again. I'm so excited by your good news.' She kissed his cheek.

'Thanks.' He grinned ruefully. 'After thirty-four years of being a bachelor I'm a bit overwhelmed by it myself.' He slid an arm about Thea's waist and drew her comfortably against him. 'Not that I didn't see it coming. As soon as I set eyes on your lovely niece, I knew my time was up.'

Thea coloured delicately. She met his teasing glance almost shyly, remembering her first day as his secretary and how he'd held her just like this to stop her flapping, and the strong attraction she'd felt for him even then. It seemed incredible that that had been only weeks ago.

'I hate to break up the party,' Melissa cut in sourly. 'But I have to be on stage at nine o'clock. Are you going to let me see Leon or not?'

'Of course.' Thea drew herself away from Matthew. 'Do you want me to come up with you?'

Melissa's mouth twisted. 'Are you afraid to trust me with my own son?'

'No, of course not. I just thought it might be better if

there was someone he knows in the room, in case he wakes up.'

Melissa's eyes darkened. 'Meaning he doesn't know me—his own mother?'

Thea saw the look of hurt in her sister's eyes and was immediately compassionate.

'Yes. But I don't mean that critically.' She put a tentative hand on her arm. 'He's only a baby, and he hasn't seen you since he was three months old. He'll probably need a little time to get used to you.'

She had expected the usual antagonism, but to her surprise Melissa merely nodded, lowering her heavy lids, hiding eyes that seemed overbright.

'Come up if you like. I'll try not to wake him. I just want to see him.'

Some of the anxiety eased out of Thea. Was it possible Melissa loved her son, after all?

The disturbing aura of Melissa's visit still clung about Thea as she stood in the kitchen, stacking dirty dishes and waiting for the coffee to percolate.

She'd been momentarily reassured by the tenderness in Melissa's face as she'd gazed at her small son, the gentleness with which she'd reached out to touch his pale, silky hair.

But it was short-lived. As she descended the stairs into the hallway, her expression changed.

'You can hang on to him a bit longer for me, can't you, Thea? I've worked so hard for this chance. I can't throw it away and take up motherhood just like that.'

'It's not a question of hanging on to Leon,' Thea said, with a feeling of hopelessness. 'You must believe I'd do that willingly.' She sighed heavily. Melissa might love Leon, but she didn't seem to understand his needs. 'You *are* his mother, Melissa. He needs you now. This first

year hasn't mattered too much. He's been loved and
cared for by Edith and me, and been quite happy. But
he's beginning to understand now. If you leave him
another year, he won't know you. He'll be used to
thinking of Edith and I as his family, and when you take
him it will be like being taken by a stranger. It's bound
to hurt him.'

Melissa's face had twisted, whether in anguish or fury,
it was difficult to tell.

'I'm late for the theatre.' she said tightly. 'I can't
discuss this now. I'll come back another time.'

She'd gone slamming off without even bothering to
say goodbye to her aunt or Matthew.

'Need a hand?' Matthew was behind her, his hands on
her waist, his lips pressing against her hair.

Thea shook off her depression and turned in his arms,
her back to the draining-board. The feel of his hard body
touching against hers sent her pulses racing madly.

'You could help me with the washing-up, if you insist.
But later. I thought we'd enjoy a cup of coffee first.'

'Wonderful idea.' His hand pushed a strand of hair
away from her cheek. 'Actually, I didn't really want to
help out, I just wanted to see you. It's damned lonely in
there without you.'

He drew her towards him and began to kiss her, tiny
arousing brushes of his lips against her sensitive mouth.

'I've been thinking about you all day.'

Thea's body shuddered in response. She'd been
thinking about him, too, and wanted nothing more than
to wrap her arms about his neck and return him kiss for
kiss. But somehow there was a restraint in her, a barrier
that was difficult to define and impossible, for the
moment, to overcome.

'The coffee's ready. I'll bring it in to you if you'll pull

up the small table ready.'

She heard him sigh, but he dropped his hands and moved away from her, leaving her to set the tray and follow him through to the sitting-room.

As she settled herself beside him, coffee-cup in hand, he sighed again.

'Is that really a cup of coffee, Thea?' he said exasperatedly. 'Or another wall I have to scale before I can reach you?'

'I don't know what you mean,' Thea said defensively.

'I think you do.'

He nibbled her ear and the cup shook in its saucer. She put it down before it spilled into her lap.

'That's better.' He settled his arm about her shoulder. 'If you're worried I'm going to make love to you, forget it. As a matter of interest, I didn't intend anticipating our wedding day, but in the circumstances prevailing at the time I'd have had to be a man of steel to resist the temptation. However, from now on I'm content to wait, as long as the wedding is soon.' He tilted her chin to look intently into her eyes. 'How about it, Thea? You could work your month's notice at the Trust, then marry me the day after you leave. Though how I'm going to keep to my vow of hands off until then, with you around me all day, I just can't imagine.'

Thea's heart pounded with excitement at the prospect he put before her. Never in her life had she wanted anything as much.

'Oh, Matthew,' she sighed, 'that would be wonderful . . .'

'But?' he prompted.

She shook her head distressfully. 'But . . . there's the problem of Leon and Melissa to be sorted out before I can even think of getting married.'

Matthew gave a deep sigh. He moved his arm from

her shoulder and sat back into the corner of the settee to survey her.

'Thea,' he said her name with slow deliberation, 'throw away your Good Samaritan hat. It's time you started thinking about yourself . . . and me.'

'Oh, Matthew!' she said ruefully. 'I can't stop worrying about Leon just like that.'

'He's Melissa's problem . . . not yours.'

Thea's hands twisted in her lap. 'I can't just abandon him to Melissa. I don't know what kind of a mother she'll be to him.'

'Neither does she,' Matthew cut in shortly. 'And she won't have a chance to find out . . . unless you give her one.'

Rita's warning, couched in almost exactly the same words, rang as an echo in Thea's head.

'Oh, God!' she whispered, sudden tears spilling on to her cheeks. 'How can I take such a risk?'

With an impatient sound, he gathered her against him.

'You have to, Thea,' he said softly. 'For Melissa and her son's sake, as well as your own.'

His hold tightened as she pressed her head into the hollow of his shoulder.

'Remember Angela?' he asked calmly. 'My sister? The photograph in the bedroom?'

Thea nodded against him.

'She's a dress designer. Quite a good one. Travels the world and wants nothing better. And that's fine . . . except that she has two children to care for. She divorced a good husband because he "crowded her space".' He made a grim sound. 'Only to find that she had to fill his space as well as her own with their children. She had to be mother and father instead of just mother.'

Thea lifted her head to look up at him, the tears drying salty and stinging on her cheeks.

'That's when she started delegating. My mother for surrogate mother and me for surrogate father . . . to her, as well as the children, most of the time. She hardly ever went home to her empty house. Why should she, when there was a room kept permanently available at a choice of two places—my flat and Mother's cottage?'

A picture of him swinging Leon easily on to his hip while he folded the pushchair rose to Thea's mind, and her heart contracted.

'You'd make such a wonderful father,' she murmured.

A grin spread across his face. 'That's something we have to discuss just as soon as we get the preliminaries of the wedding over.

He lowered his head and his mouth covered hers lingeringly, making her head whirl. Her hand crept up around his back, but he removed it with a shake of his head.

'No more distractions. I haven't finished my lecture. The crunch came when she began on her liaisons. One disreputable type after another. It was then that Mother and I decided that enough was enough, and gave her back the job of looking after her own children. Time and energy-consuming enough to keep her out of any really damaging mischief. She performed, at first, pretty much as Melissa has and will, but she got used to it. She might not admit it to anyone but herself, but it's obvious she finds it a more satisfying life than racketing around looking for something to fill the gap.'

A ray of hope stirred in Thea. 'Do you think the same thing will happen to Melissa?'

He shrugged. 'I can't be sure. It's a gamble, but if it doesn't work we'll still be around to pick up the pieces for Leon.'

'Persuading Melissa it's for her own good and not just spite won't be easy,' she said doubtfully.

'You'll do it,' he said, adding with a teasing grin, 'She's not the only family member with determination. But call me in as rearguard if you need one.'

Thea sighed and leaned her head against his chest, listening to the strong momentum of his heart. 'Oh, Matthew, you're such a comfort.'

'Comfort?' he said, the sound reverberating against her eardrum. 'You make me sound like a woolly bedsock. One more remark like that, young lady, and I'll have to forget my own embargo and prove to you that I can be much more exciting than a dozen bedsocks.'

She gave him a sly look that was more than half pleading.

'I wish you would.'

But he shook his head firmly. 'The wedding first.' His hand moved tantalisingly across her breasts, creating a tremor along her nervous system. 'Now I know I've got a carrot to dangle in front of your unwilling nose, I'm going to use it to the full, with a few enticing examples of what you're going to be missing while you make up your mind.'

CHAPTER TEN

'DAMN! Damn! Damn!'

Thea swore aloud as she slammed each drawer of her desk shut.

'I know I put it in one of these drawers.'

Three hectic days of dictation and transcription—vanished into thin air.

'Can I come in?'

Thea looked up and groaned. Rita stood in the office doorway, an unusually hesitant look on her face.

'Do you come as friend or foe?' Thea's question was only half joking. Over the past weeks, she and Rita seemed to have drifted apart, the old camaraderie lost in the general air of Rita's critical disapproval.

'Friend, of course. What else?'

Rita sounded affronted, and there was a faint flush beneath her fair skin.

'I was beginning to wonder.'

Thea watched in dismay as Rita's face darkened.

'Oh, for goodness' sake, Rita, don't go all huffy on me again. Come in. I need a second opinion.'

Rita relaxed and came into the room, shutting the door behind her.

'Matthew about?'

'No. He's in Wales.' Did her chagrin show? Thea wondered. The first three days of the week had been taken up with the notes and reports on the Moroccan loan and, true to his word, Matthew had hardly even touched her.

Yesterday and today he'd been in Wales, and ten

minutes ago he'd phoned to remind her that he would be paying a visit to his home village to see his mother and to make arrangements for their wedding, which they'd both agreed should take place in his picturesque local church.

'That second opinion you mentioned?' Rita cut into her thoughts. 'I think you should know. I'm not medically qualified.'

Thea laughed. It was good to have the old Rita back. The question was, how long would it last when she heard the news? Oh, well, she would most probably be past caring by then.

'I think I'm going mad,' she said, her smile fading as she remembered. 'I put the Moroccan file in one of these drawers just before I went for coffee . . . and it's vanished.' She chewed her lip in vexation. 'Do I look psychotic to you?'

Rita studied her for a few seconds and then said wryly, 'A bit ragged around the edges perhaps, but I'd say you were sane enough.'

'Thanks.' Thea sighed. 'But seriously, an important file's gone missing and this isn't the first time it's happened.'

'Is that why you're leaving?'

The question fell softly between them, momentarily suspending Thea's breath. She let it out slowly.

'Linda Prosser was instructed to keep it quiet,' she said grimly.

Rita shrugged. 'It doesn't have to be Linda. It's a fact that walls have ears.'

Thea grunted disgustedly. 'Who told you?'

'What does it matter?' Rita's smile was cynical. 'It's an item on the grapevine news sheet.'

'What else does it say?'

'Is there anything else to say?' Rita grinned slyly.

'Would you care to make a statement?'

'No, I wouldn't.'

Thea felt irritated. It shouldn't matter. People would know eventually anyway, but it was galling, nevertheless. She could well imagine the gossip and speculation. It was probably being given about that yet another of Matthew Clayburn's secretaries had failed the acid test.

She was half tempted to confide in Rita the real reason for her resignation, if only to have the satisfaction of being the one to give the true version, but she and Matthew had decided to withhold the news until the last minute.

Rita's hand fell on Thea's arm and her brown eyes were full of sympathy.

'I'm really sorry, Thea. I know I teased you a bit at first, but underneath I felt that if anyone could make the grade, it would be you.' She screwed up her face in disgust. 'It just goes to show how impossible a man he is.'

Thea had to bite her tongue to keep from rushing to Matthew's defence, but managed instead a non-committal smile.

Rita was, she knew, only exhibiting her loyalty to a friend. If the news of her resignation really was all over the building, then she might have to put up with quite a bit more of the same from her friendlier colleagues, and possibly some open sniping from less friendly quarters.

Oh, well, she thought resignedly. She could enjoy the thought of the surprise that was in store for friend and foe alike when the news of her wedding to Matthew Clayburn finally came out.

She spent the rest of the afternoon searching for the missing file in every nook and cranny of her office and, in desperation, Matthew's also, although she knew it couldn't be in there.

Fortunately, the concise and extremely lengthy report was on the computer, but it would take a full day to print up another copy. She would have to wait until Monday to do it.

It was another irritation to add to her disappointment over the lonely weekend ahead. Matthew had promised to pop in late on Sunday evening, but even that was spoilt by the thought of having to tell him another file had gone missing.

As soon as she opened the front door, she noticed the change in atmosphere. The usually calm, welcoming air of home was charged with an electricity that could only be Melissa. The strong, sweet perfume wafting from the living-room confirmed Thea's supposition.

Melissa was sitting on the settee, a solemn and obviously awed Leon perched on her fashionably skirted knee.

'Hello, Melissa.'

'Hello, Thea.'

The small ray of hope which had begun to burn at the homely scene before her disappeared in the light of Melissa's set and unfriendly expression.

'As instructed, I've come.'

'So I see.' Thea swallowed a sigh. 'And I'm glad, because we've a lot to discuss.'

Edith came in from the kitchen. 'If you've finished with Leon, I'll put him to bed before we have dinner.'

She patted Thea's arm in passing. 'Do you think we could leave the discussion until after we've eaten?'

Thea nodded. But, judging from Melissa's face, the signals were stormy and she doubted if she'd manage to eat much with the obvious battle ahead hanging over her.

Melissa was also obviously feeling the strain. She

pushed her food about on her plate, but ate very little of it. At last, as though she could bear the delay no longer, she looked directly and challengingly at Thea.

'Well, what have you decided?'

'Decided? Me?' Thea looked startled.

'Yes. With my future hanging in the balance, I'd like to know if you've decided to help me or to destroy my chances of being a success.'

Thea's first reaction was one of guilt. She'd been her sister's keeper for so long, it was almost automatic to put herself and her own needs second to those of Melissa. But this wasn't simply a question between the two of them. There was Leon's future to consider, and that was more important than anything.

'I take it, then, that you don't want Leon?' She was surprised at the steadiness in her voice, when her insides were churning.

Melissa's face flooded with angry colour.

'Typical of you to make a statement like that,' she said harshly. 'Everything's in black and white for you, isn't it, Thea? Either . . . or. No alternatives.'

Thea's own anger rose, washing away her guilt.

'Perhaps that's because there aren't any alternatives. Leon's your child, he needs you. It's time you took responsibility for him, before it's too late.'

'Thea,' Edith broke in quietly, 'does it have to be now? Couldn't I just go on looking after Leon until Melissa is ready to take him?'

Thea felt as though the ground had been cut from under her feet. It struck her suddenly and forcibly that she had forgotten to take into consideration her aunt's vested interest. She didn't *want* Leon to go.

Her face softened with compassion. It was really one more reason why this had to be settled now. The longer Edith had the care of Leon, the more deeply she would be hurt by their parting.

'Leon is Melissa's child, Edith,' she said gently. 'It's time she started thinking of herself as his mother. She can't go on expecting other people to shoulder her responsibilities.' She thought of Matthew and his dilemma with his own sister, and stiffened her resolve. 'I'm only trying to do what's best for her and for Leon.'

'Hah!'

Melissa's harsh exclamation jerked Thea's attention back to her.

'Thea, the all-knowing one . . . the fount of all wisdom.'

Melissa's eyes blazed.

'How I always hated being told by Mummy—go to Thea . . . ask Thea . . . Thea knows. How often have I been sick to death of Thea?'

Thea stared, her heart pounding uncomfortably as sudden memories came thick and fast . . . and with them a new insight. How often had *she* been sick of her mother's insistence that she take Melissa with her practically everywhere she went. Once, when she'd protested that she didn't want Melissa's constant company, her mother had been sadly reproachful.

'Melissa is your sister, Thea. The best friend you'll ever have in life. You should cherish her.'

The reproach had left Thea feeling selfish and guilty, and the feeling had become deeply entrenched, arising almost automatically whenever she was tempted to put her own interests first. Now she saw that, probably with the best of intentions, her mother had forced a closeness between her two daughters which had made it virtually impossible for them to be friends.

Some of Thea's antagonism faded.

'I know just how you feel,' she said ruefully. 'I was just as sick of having *you* thrust on me every minute of the day. It looks as though we've both had a rough time of it.'

Thea's smile brought an answering one from Melissa. 'Then you do understand, Thea?' Melissa said coaxingly. 'You will help by keeping Leon for me?'

Thea made a small sound of exasperation. This was how it had always been, too. Melissa's eyes, liquid and pleading, had always been able to melt Thea's heart.

But a small shred of resistance remained.

'I'm getting married in less than a month, Melissa,' she said gently. 'Things have changed and we have to sort out the problem of Leon now.'

'Ah, yes!' Melissa's smile vanished. 'To the wonderful Mr Clayburn! And obviously, he doesn't want the inconvenience of a bastard in the family.'

Thea gasped with shock, and Edith, who had been sitting quietly between them, echoed her dismay.

'Melissa! How can you say such a thing?'

Thea said stiffly, 'I'm sure the question of whether Leon knows his father or not has never entered Matthew's head. As a matter of fact, he loves Leon, and if you really don't want him, we'd be very happy to adopt him.'

'Oh, I'm sure!' Melissa sneered, an ugly light gleaming in her eyes. 'You'd like that, wouldn't you . . . to take away the only thing that's ever truly been mine?'

Thea caught her breath in a deep sigh and closed her eyes despairingly. Melissa's mind was a maze. No matter which way you turned, it led only to a blocked ending.

'You can't have it all ways, Melissa,' she said faintly.

'Can't I?' Melissa's voice was thick with venom. 'Perhaps I can. Perhaps Matthew Clayburn is marrying the wrong Lawson. If he wants Leon . . . it could be arranged . . . legally.'

Thea stared, suddenly frightened by the malice which faced her across the dinner-table.

'What do you mean?'

'I mean, my dear Thea, that your fiancé should be marrying me . . . the mother of his child. Leon's father is Matthew Clayburn.'

Thea's shock left her speechless and faint.

Edith said thickly, 'For shame, Melissa! What are you saying?'

'I'm saying,' Melissa replied with emphasis, 'that one year and nine months ago, Matthew Clayburn and I met at a theatre party. Afterwards, he took me home to my hotel room and made love to me. Leon is the product of that one-night stand.'

It was an awful weekend. Thea wondered how she managed to go through the motions. Matthew had suggested that she take the opportunity to do some weekend shopping for her trousseau, insisting generously that she charge everything to him. Like an automaton, she did so, and afterwards was at a loss to remember what she had bought.

Not that it mattered, she thought hopelessly, since, if what Melissa had said was true, she wouldn't be wearing any of it. If it was true, she couldn't, in all fairness, blame Matthew. He couldn't be held responsible to her for what he'd done nearly two years ago. But if he was Leon's father it would create problems which would make it impossible for them to marry.

Sunday evening came at last and Thea sat by the window, watching for Matthew's car. She both longed for and dreaded to see it pulling up outside of the house. When it did, dread took the upper hand.

On leaden feet, she went to let him in.

The light of anticipation in his eyes dimmed when

he saw her expression.

He dropped a kiss lightly on her lips and then grimaced as she responded woodenly, standing back quickly to let him pass into the hall.

'Problems?' He hooked his arm about her rigid shoulders. 'Don't tell me, let me guess. It's Melissa.'

'Yes,' Thea confirmed tightly as she led the way into the living-room. 'Leon's in bed and Aunt Edith's gone out.' She sat on the settee. 'Matthew, we have to talk.'

He sat down beside her, drawing away into the corner of the settee so that he could see her face.

'OK,' he said guardedly. 'Fire away.'

Thea twisted her skirt in nervous fingers to stop them from visibly shaking.

'Matthew,' she began, unable to meet his questioning eyes, 'did you meet Melissa at a theatre party nearly two years ago?'

'I think the anwser to that is yes. At first, I wasn't sure where I'd met her before, but I'm sure now that I did.'

Thea caught her lower lip between her teeth, unable for the moment to go on, but she had to know.

'Did you sleep with her?'

There was a pause and then he said, 'Did she say that I did?'

Thea nodded. 'Yes.'

She heard him sigh deeply and looked up. He met her anxious gaze squarely.

'If she says I did, then it's entirely likely.'

'Oh, my God!' Thea buried her face in her hands.

With an exasperated sound, Matthew reached suddenly for her hands and held them firmly against her attempt to pull away. He looked at the tears running down her cheeks and groaned. 'For heaven's sake, Thea, it's an unfortunate thing to have happened . . . but damn it all . . . I couldn't have known then that I would meet and fall in love with the girl's sister.'

Thea swallowed a sob and drew and deep, shuddering breath. 'Matthew, Melissa says you're Leon's father,' Thea cried into the shocked silence. 'Oh, Matthew! What are we going to do?'

Almost absently, he gathered her to him, pressing her head against his chest.

'Hush, Thea. I have to think.'

Thea muffled her sobs in the hollow of his shoulder.

'Leon doesn't have the Clayburn eyes,' he said at last, and then added almost to himself, 'But I don't suppose that would be inevitable.'

'He has blue eyes,' Thea sniffed, and sat up. 'But not your cornflower-blue shade.'

Matthew's mouth twisted. 'My mother's eyes are brown, like Angela's. I suppose it's possible for the mixture to be muted to a cooler blue.'

Thea gasped. 'Matthew, do you think it might be true?'

His face was grim. 'Anything's possible. What we have to do is find out for certain. Where's Melissa? At the theatre?'

'No.' She shook her head. 'There's no performance today. And I don't know where she's staying.'

'Tomorrow, then,' Matthew said determinedly. 'She'll be at the theatre tomorrow and so will we.'

The doorbell rang loudly.

Thea frowned. 'Aunt Edith must have forgotten her key.' She dabbed at her eyes with the back of her hand and stood up. 'I'll go and let her in.'

'Hello, Thea.' Melissa confronted Thea on the doorstep, a suitcase in each hand. 'May I come in?'

'Of course,' Thea said faintly and stood back to let her sister pass.

'Thank you.' Melissa smiled sweetly. 'After all, this is

my home as much as yours, Mum and Dad left it to us equally.'

She dropped the cases in the hall and made for the living-room.

Thea's heart began to hammer as she followed her sister's determined figure into the living-room. She had a horrible feeling that, from today, her life would change irrevocably.

'Hello, Matthew,' Melissa said cheerfully. 'Did Thea tell you my news?'

Matthew had risen and his eyes narrowed on Melissa's triumphant face.

'Yes, she told me. We've just been discussing it.'

'Of course,' she agreed, seating herself on the vacated settee. 'And what have you decided?'

'This isn't a game, Melissa. Leon's a human being, not a pawn.' Matthew grimaced impatiently. 'You must realise that I shall want proof.'

Melissa's plucked brows rose and she smiled. 'You mean blood tests, I suppose?'

Matthew nodded. 'Unless you know of some less painful way of finding out the truth.'

'I don't, but that's beside the point. There will be no blood tests and no proof. You'll just have to take my word for it. And I say you're Leon's father.'

'Don't be ridiculous,' Thea cut in, angered by the smug satisfaction on Melissa's face. 'Surely you can't expect Matthew to take responsibility for Leon until he knows for sure that he's his father.'

'I'm not asking your precious fiancé to take responsibility for anything. And I don't want anything from him, not for Leon nor for myself. I've managed this far without him and I intend to go on doing so.' Melissa's smile vanished, in its place a heavy scowl. 'I know the truth. You and your Mr Clayburn will just have to learn to live with the fact that he'll never be sure.'

'You're evil, Melissa.' Thea's voice shook. 'You must hate me a great deal.'

Melissa nodded. 'Yes. I think I must.'

Matthew's arm came about Thea's shoulder and she leaned against him weakly.

'I don't think there's anything more to gain from this discussion, Thea. We'll talk about it together when Melissa has left.'

Melissa's smile was back. 'Oh, but I'm not going. I've decided to do as my sister asks and take responsibility for my son. From now on, I intend to live at home and look after him. I'm sure Aunt Edith will be only too delighted to help out with him when I'm at the theatre.'

CHAPTER ELEVEN

'COME home with me tonight, Thea.' Matthew stopped by Thea's desk and looked at her with a crease between his brows. 'We have to talk.'

Thea nodded resignedly. 'We could go straight from the office, if you don't think my getting into your car in the car park might cause too big a stir.'

It had been an attempt at levity which misfired.

Matthew's frown deepened. 'I think there are more important things to worry about than the Trust grapevine.'

His face looked tight and drawn, and Thea guessed her own expression would be showing similar signs of strain.

Since Sunday night, when Melissa's bombshell had been dropped on Matthew's head, they'd had hardly a minute to themselves. The missing file had put Thea behind with her work. She'd had to spend all day Monday making up a new file, and everything else had accumulated.

In between times, when Matthew wasn't dictating, he was involved in the usual round of meetings and negotiations, and Thea had seen little of him.

When she'd presented him with the newly printed Moroccan file, with an apology for its late completion, he had hardly seemed to hear her explanation, appearing deeply preoccupied with his inner thoughts. Thea guessed they would include the problem of Leon's paternity.

She rang Edith to tell her she wouldn't be home for

dinner. Her aunt sounded cheerful

'I won't hold dinner for you, then, dear. Have a nice evening and try to relax.'

Since Melissa had moved in, her aunt had seemed almost happier than before. Perhaps having Melissa on the spot removed the fear that she might appear at any time and snatch Leon from Edith's arms.

Ironically, Melissa's luck had taken an upward swing. Her performance in the farce had been acclaimed by the critics and she'd been elated by an unexpected request to appear on a television magazine programme to talk about herself.

Edith was equally thrilled, since it meant Melissa's mothering role was, so far, merely a token one.

From time to time, her aunt's sympathetic eyes rested on Thea, inviting her confidence, but for the moment it seemed impossible to talk about her feelings, still raw and uncertain, with anyone—not even Matthew.

But, from the determined look on Matthew's face, her evasions were at an end. Tonight she would be forced to put into words her nebulous fears about their future together. She still loved him and the thought of not marrying him, after all, was incredibly painful. But would it be any more painful than marrying and then living with the uncertainty about whether he was the father of her sister's child?

Tears pricked the back of her eyes. 'I thought it was all too good to be true,' she muttered miserably. At the back of her mind had been the age-old fear of tempting fate with too much happiness.

It was the longest day she'd ever known, and wasted from the point of view of getting anything done. She couldn't settle to any of the numerous tasks piling up so alarmingly; her concentration was practically nil and by five-thirty she had a headache from frustration and worry.

Matthew's buzzer sounded and she went into his room with the feeling of a condemned man meeting his fate. Because, at some time during the interminable afternoon, she had decided she couldn't marry him until the question of Leon's paternity had been proved or disproved. And, since she knew Melissa's stubborn spite was impervious to reason, she had resigned herself to telling Matthew that she couldn't marry him.

'Thea, come in. I'm almost ready to go.' He looked up at her and frowned. 'You're as white as a sheet.'

He came around the desk and put his arms about her.

Thea pushed at him gently, disentangling herself from his arms.

'It's no use, Matthew. I can't marry you. Not with this thing hanging over our heads.'

She saw the colour drain away from his face.

'You're not going to let your sister spoil things between us?'

Thea swallowed the lump in her throat. 'I can't help it. No matter how much I tell myself I understand, I still can't forget that you did sleep with Melissa and that Leon's the outcome.'

Matthew's colour came back in a surge.

'I can't say I blame you for the way you feel.' He rubbed his long fingers against the sides of his temples. 'Oh, God! If only I could remember.'

He moved away from Thea and went to stand at the window, gazing unseeingly out.

'I've thought about it long and hard, and I remember Melissa and the occasion. I was stupid enough to put money into a theatre production and then was bulldozed into going along to the celebration party after the show. It wasn't my scene at all, and I'd already had a pretty trying day at the office. I suppose I drank rather more than I usually do.'

He turned back to Thea, a frown of concentration on his wide brow.

'Somebody introduced me to your sister, and I remember thinking she was far too young to be so drunk. It was obvious she would need help to get home, so I offered to take her by taxi. It was a good excuse to leave the party early.' He shrugged. 'Melissa seemed quite happy with the arrangement, and when we reached her hotel she asked me if I'd come in and make her a cup of strong black coffee. So I did.'

Thea's knees felt suddenly weak, and she sat shakily on a nearby chair.

'What happened then?' she prompted, not sure she wanted to hear the answer.

Matthew shook his head. 'That's when it all begins to go hazy. I remember making the coffee. And I remember Melissa kissing me.'

Thea's stomach clenched. *'She* kissed *you?'*

Matthew nodded, seeming not to notice the hint of sarcasm in Thea's voice.

'Yes. With a kind of desperation, actually. I remember feeling sorry for her.'

'And at that point you took her to bed to console her?' Thea's voice broke. 'For God's sake, Matthew! She was barely eighteen.'

'Yes, I know.' His face darkened. 'And, despite my lurid reputation—highly exaggerated, I might add— seducing drunken eighteen-year-olds is definitely not my style.' His mouth twisted cynically. 'If I did it, then I don't remember having the satisfaction. I must have drunk more champagne than I'd realised.'

'You . . . don't remember . . . making love?' Thea's voice shook.

'No. After the coffee and the kisses, all I remember is

waking up in the early hours of the morning, surprised to find myself lying, stiff and cold, on the settee of a strange hotel.'

'And Melissa?' Thea's question was hardly more than a whisper.

'She was in the kitchen making more coffee when I came around. The rattle of cups must have roused me.' Matthew groaned and sank down at his desk, his face hidden in his hands. 'I can't tell you how I felt when she told me what had happened . . . that we'd made love on the carpet before I'd fallen asleep.'

Thea sat quietly, her heart heavy, her mind searching for reassurance. 'Melissa wouldn't lie,' she said shakily. 'Not about you . . . and she . . . and Leon! Not about something as important as that.'

Matthew's fist hit the desk, startling Thea's heart into an uncomfortable thudding.

'Melissa's got to agree to Leon having those blood tests,' he said. 'I've got a distinctive blood group which should settle matters pretty conclusively. It's the only way we're going to know for sure.'

Thea shook her head. 'She won't agree. I know Melissa and she's immovable, especially when she's got the upper hand.'

Matthew came around the desk and took her hands gently in his, pulling her to her feet.

'Look, Thea, I can't pretend this stupid mess doesn't make some difference, because obviously it does, but I don't honestly see why it should change the way things are with you and I in the long run. I love you. I want to marry you. Let's take it from there.'

He stepped closer, tilting her chin so that she was forced to look into his dazzling eyes.

'Have you stopped loving me, Thea?'

With a sob, Thea moved forward into his arms, clinging to him in a strange desperation. 'You know I haven't.'

'Do I?' he said softly. 'Prove it to me.'

His head dipped suddenly and his mouth covered hers possessively.

The effect was instant and inevitable. Thea's arms went up about his neck, her fingers tangling in his hair, drawing him closer, her hungry lips finding nectar.

His hands swept with an equal hunger along the length of her spine, into the curve of her waist and down over her hips, moulding her against him, sending flames of desire licking through her body.

'I've waited a long time for you to come along, my darling,' he said fiercely against her mouth. 'And I won't have you snatched away from me by a spoiled brat who is going to listen to reason if I have to beat her into it.'

A huge sigh shook Thea, and the fire in her veins subsided. He felt the wane of her desire and loosened his hold on her.

'No one's ever been able to beat Melissa into anything,' she said sadly.

'Well, I'm going to try,' he replied grimly, putting her from him. 'Change of plan. We're going to your place to see if we can't catch the little madam before she leaves for the theatre. Perhaps a threat to tie her up and keep her from her performance might be some help.'

Thea laughed, and then saw that he was more than half serious.

'There probably won't be any dinner. I've already phoned Aunt Edith to say I wouldn't be eating at home.'

'No problem. When we've finished with Melissa, we can go out to dinner by way of a victory celebration.'

Thea bit her lip. Matthew might yet learn a thing or two about determination when he tangled with Melissa, but there didn't seem to be any point in warning him of that.

'I haven't finished locking up yet,' she said. 'Now that files seem to be going missing again, I have to be doubly careful about that.' She shook her head in perplexity. 'You don't think they could be being stolen by a competitor, do you?' She was only half joking.

'Unlikely,' Matthew said shortly. 'But let's deal with one problem at a time.'

He shrugged into his jacket.

'I'll go down and bring the car around to the front of the building while you lock up. If we leave it much later we might just miss that sister of yours, and the way I feel, I couldn't stand the strain of waiting for her to come back home tonight.'

He rushed out, leaving his own cabinets and desk drawers unlocked and, with a sigh, Thea set about checking the safety precautions and straightening his desk. His briefcase, which he'd left on his desk, she picked up to put away in the safe.

A sound next door stayed her hand on the combination lock.

'Matthew, is that you? You were quick.'

There was no reply.

She finished putting the case in the safe and walked towards her own room. A funny, acrid smell hung in the air. It alerted the nerves on the back of her neck and she rushed forward.

Muriel was bending over the large metal waste-bin which was now full of files and which burned as she fanned the already fierce flames. There was a pool of liquid on the floor and as Thea stood, rooted to the spot with horror, Muriel kicked over the bin and the flames shot across the carpet, creating a barrier between herself and Thea.

There was a strange smile on her lips and her eyes

were wide and very bright.

'Not so much a blushing bride, as a burning one.'

And, as Thea rushed forward in an attempt to push through the flames, Muriel ran to the door, and pulled it open and, with a last triumphant look at the bewildered Thea, slammed it behind her. Thea heard the turning of the key above the roaring of her heartbeat.

She cleared the spreading flames with a wild leap, and managed to get to the door. It was locked, and she wrenched at the handle with futile strength.

'Matthew!' she screamed, knowing he wouldn't hear. He was probably sitting outside in the car, wondering impatiently what was taking her so long.

The room was full of flames and a dark, billowing smoke.

'Matthew!' she choked, her voice barely audible over the roar of the fire and her own coughing.

Oh, God! Help me! Thea prayed, but already she could feel the wrenching suffocation of her lungs and knew it was useless. She sank slowly to the floor, her hands covering her nose and mouth in an attempt to protect herself from the penetrating fumes and smoke.

And then suddenly the door was opening and strong arms were dragging her out of the room.

'Thea! Oh, my God! Thea! Are you still conscious?' Matthew's voice was ragged with panic. 'Stay there one second while I sound the alarm.'

Thea lay huddled in the corridor, unable to move, until the sound of a bell rang through the building and Matthew was back, lifting her up into his arms.

'How did you know I was in danger?' Thea's voice was a croak, still raw from the stinging effect of the smoke and fumes.

She was sitting propped on cushions on the settee, a

blanket across her knees, and a mug of hot, sweet tea clutched in still-shaking hands.

Matthew's expression was black with anger, although he still had the pallor of shock.

'I was standing beside the car, wondering what was keeping you so long, when Muriel rushed out of the front of the building. She froze when she saw me and then laughed, shouting something about having a funeral instead of a wedding. I didn't stop to ask what she meant, I just grabbed her, gave her to Joe in the foyer and ran. The look on her face was enough to convince me she was serious.'

He took the mug from Thea's hand and held her against him.

'When we're married, I intend to lock you up and only let you out when I'm around to look after you. Those nine lives are running dangerously low.'

Thea cuddled against him, knowing nothing on earth was going to keep her now from marrying him. Suddenly, even the problem of Melissa and Leon had lost its power to hurt. Nothing mattered against the awful fact that she could have died without ever knowing the true depth of their love. 'I don't mind anything . . . as long as you *do* marry me soon.'

He leaned away from her and tilted her chin. 'And if we never do find out the truth about Leon?'

Thea shrugged. 'It doesn't matter. We'll all be part of the same family, anyway. I don't mind Melissa having her small triumph, as long as I have you.'

Matthew gave a deep sigh and his wonderful eyes lit up.

'I'm almost grateful to Muriel for putting the damned business into its proper perspective.'

Thea chewed her lip. 'What will happen to Muriel?'

The last thing she'd seen as Matthew carried her out

through the foyer of the building was Muriel's frightened face as she stood where Matthew had left her, in the firm grasp of the porter at reception, with the loud clanging of the fire engines arriving outside to add to the nightmare.

Matthew shrugged. 'I don't know. Fortunately, you're safe and the damage to the building isn't too extensive. But don't let's talk about that now. I just want to savour the fact that you're here . . . safe in my arms.'

'Oh, Matthew!' Thea lifted her lips for his kiss.

Edith came in much later to find them sitting contentedly in each other's arms.

'It's wonderful to see you both so happy again.' She smiled. 'You've no idea how unhappy my poor Thea has been this past week.'

Matthew grunted. 'Oh, yes, I have. I've been pretty unhappy myself, you know.'

'Of course you have. How silly of me.' Edith kissed his cheek in reparation. 'I know you'll both be so good together, and there's all the time in the world to make it up to each other.'

The front door opened and banged shut, and there was the sound of raised voices in the hall.

Melissa came into the room, her face like thunder. 'Now you're here, you'd better come in.'

A tall, rangy young man entered behind her, his face almost as angry as Melissa's, but she made no attempt to introduce him.

'Oh, God! The whole bloody family's here,' he exploded. 'I want to speak to you, Melissa. Is there somewhere we could go?'

Melissa tossed her jacket on the back of an armchair and sank inelegantly into it, kicking off her shoes.

'The family, as you so inaptly put it, can hear what

you have to say. They'll hear it eventually, anyway.'

'OK—if that's the way you want it.' He towered over her. 'Why the hell did you unload that bombshell on to me and then disappear? Didn't you think I had any right to know what happened to my child?'

Thea and Matthew, who had been watching the exchange in fascination, looked at one another before Matthew's eyes narrowed on Melissa. She had a funny, twisted smile on her lips.

'You weren't interested then. Why should you be now?'

Two bright spots of anger showed on the young man's cheeks.

'Interested? Hell, I was stunned. Here was I, just about to go off to America for a lucrative tour, and you calmly tell me you're pregnant. What reaction did you expect?' He glowered at her. 'You might at least have given me a day or two to get used to the idea of being a father. I was frantic when I found you'd gone off. No one knew where. And I had to go with the group on that bloody tour, which should have been the triumph of our careers, with a thing like that hanging over me. I swore I'd find you when I got back, even if only to pay you back for that.' His lips curled cynically. 'Did you think you could fool me by changing your name? I knew you as soon as I saw that stupid face of yours on television. Did you think I wouldn't?'

'I didn't care,' Melissa flung at him. 'I changed my name to change my luck, not because of you. I didn't give you a thought, you'll be devastated to know.'

He grinned nastily. 'Somehow I doubt that. But then, you always were an egotistical, self-centred little cow. Quite frankly, I don't know why I bothered with you in the first place.'

'And why are you bothering now? My son and I

don't need you.'

A bemused expression crossed his face. 'We had a son?'

'Not we,' Melissa corrected sarcastiscally. '*I* had a son.'

He lunged and pulled her to her feet, shaking her until the teeth rattled in her head.

'He's my son, too. And you're going to listen to reason.'

'I wouldn't bank on it.' Matthew's dry voice cut across the altercation. 'Reason seems not to be one of Melissa's strong points. And neither is truth.'

He disentangled them, pushing Melissa back into her seat and indicated a nearby armchair to the irate stranger.

'But that doesn't mean this matter can't be sorted out amicably.'

'Thea.' Melissa's face appeared, unusually hesitant, around the door. 'Can I come in?'

Thea's brows rose in mock surprise. 'So polite! That's not like you. Are you ill?'

Thea had seen little of Melissa over the past day or so, which had been a relief. She was still trying to come to terms with the depth of her fury.

'Thea, please.' Melissa perched on the end of the bed as Thea continued doggedly with her packing. 'I want to apologise.'

Thea folded her lips. 'That isn't like you, either.'

'Oh, for God's sake!' Melissa stood up and began to pace the room. 'Haven't you ever done something you regret? I was miserable. Rikki's tour of America was a huge sucess. He'd made a lot of money and I had nothing but his son. I was determined I'd make a success of my own career, even if only to prove to him that I didn't need him. I did make a success and it should have been wonderful, but it wasn't. I still wanted Rikki and I missed Leon, but there didn't seem to be much I could do about it.'

She stopped pacing and looked at Thea. 'Then you turned up and forced me to come and see Leon, and it brought back all the heartache I thought I'd conquered. I'd lost Rikki and you had Matthew. I couldn't bear to see you so sickeningly happy.'

'So you set out deliberately to ruin it with a vicious lie.' Thea's voice shook with the fury and uncertainty she'd been desperately trying to bury. 'I want you to tell me the truth, Melissa. Did Matthew sleep with you?'

Two bright spots of colour appeared on Melissa's cheeks.

'No,' she said after a pause. 'He didn't.' Her mouth twisted bitterly. 'Can you imagine it? He wasn't interested! In me! There was I, all panting passion . . . and the man falls asleep. I had to tell him we'd done it . . . to save my pride.' She smiled sourly. 'At the time it did no one any harm. I dare say it boosted his ego.'

Thea burned with a painful mixture of relief and anger.

'Of course, you would see it that way.' Thea had never felt more like hitting her sister. She clenched her itching hands to keep them still. 'Melissa! Why did you do such a wicked thing?'

Melissa shrugged. 'Rikki didn't turn up at the theatre party. I wanted to spite him.'

Thea shook her head unbelievingly. 'You were sleeping with Rikki at the time? Did you know then you were pregnant?'

Melissa shook her head. 'Not for definite.'

A painful thought arose in Thea's mind. 'Did you plan to sleep with another man so you could later blame him for your pregnancy?'

'Even I'm not that devious!' Melissa snorted inelegantly. 'No, it was all done on the spur of the moment.'

Thea hesitated before asking her next question.

'I suppose you *are* sure Rikki is Leon's father?'

Melissa's laugh held genuine amusement. 'Of course. You're not very observant, are you? Leon is a replica of his father.'

Thea let out a long, shaky breath. 'Yes. Now you mention it, I suppose he is.'

Melissa's mouth twisted. 'That's why he's so bloody smug and pleased with himself. You'd think from the way he's carrying on, he'd given birth himself. He wants us to get married . . . go and live in his posh house and be one big, happy family.' She paused and looked soberly at her sister. 'Thea, do you think I should do it?'

Thea laughed bitterly. 'You're asking me? Thea . . . the all-knowing one? The one you hate and tried to destroy?'

To Thea's surprise, Melissa burst into tears. Habit died hard, and Thea found herself gathering her sister against her.

'I didn't really hate you, Thea. I admired you. Looked up to you. But Mummy always going on about you made me feel inadequate. I vowed then I'd do something one day to make her see I could be special, too.'

Thea's anger faded. 'Oh, Melissa! You always were special. To all of us. And I'm proud of you for getting where you are, without any help from anyone . . . I really am.'

Melissa lifted her head from Thea's shoulder and sniffed. 'Then *you* don't hate *me*.'

'I don't hate you. It hasn't always been easy to love you, but somehow I've managed it.' She wiped a tear from her sister's cheek with a gentle finger. 'Do you still love Rikki?'

Melissa snorted. 'Yes. I suppose I do. God knows why.'

'Then give him a whirl.'

Melissa moved restlessly. 'I want it all, Thea. I don't want to give up my career . . . not even for Leon.'

'Then take Aunt Edith with you. She'd adore to look after Leon for you. She's dying a thousand deaths worrying she may never see him again.'

Melissa's face lit up with a brilliant smile. 'What a wonderful idea! Now why didn't I think of that? Perhaps Mum was right, after all—you really do know a thing or two.'

She gave Thea the first spontaneous hug she could remember having, and it brought tears to her eyes.

'I really am sorry for all the awful things I've done to you. I'll try to find a way to make it up to you.'

'You look after Leon and be happy. Believe it or not, that's all I've ever wanted for you both.'

'I know.' Melissa kissed Thea's cheek. 'Thanks. Now I'll leave you to your packing.'

Thea nodded. 'Perhaps you'd better . . . if I'm ever to be ready in time.'

After Melissa left, she heaved a sigh of relief. At least that was one problem which seemed to be solved.

Matthew had insisted she take the week off from work. The office was in chaos anyway, with workmen all over the place carrying out emergency repairs to the fire damage, and it was unlikely anything worth while would be accomplished in the mess. She'd spent the week trying to wind down.

The trauma of the fire had subsided in her mind, until now it seemed more in the nature of a bad dream than a reality. Thea wondered, not for the first time, how

184 A QUESTION OF TRUST

Muriel had known she and Matthew were to be married. But now, along with everything else, it didn't seem to matter.

All that mattered was that very soon she would be Mrs Matthew Clayburn. She shivered with pleasure at the thought, but it was closely followed by a new anxiety.

Matthew had insisted that she go with him this weekend to his mother's cottage.

'Give my family a chance to look you over,' he'd said teasingly. 'But I should warn you, my mother thinks no woman is good enough for her handsome son.'

Thea had snorted in disgust. 'Then no wonder her son has grown up so arrogant and conceited.'

He'd kissed her breathless as a punishment for that, but it hadn't removed the anxiety.

'What if your mother really doesn't like me?' she'd murmured doubtfully.

'Then I'll marry you, anyway,' he'd responded solemnly, and then, seeing the distress on her face, he relented. 'Stop worrying, Thea. She'll find you adorable, just as I do.'

'Thea.' Edith came into the bedroom just as Thea was snapping shut the locks on her case. 'Rita's called to see you. I've put her in the sitting-room.'

'I hope I haven't called at an awkward time,' Rita said, with unfamiliar humility.

'It's all right. Matthew won't be here for another half an hour or so. Would you like a cup of coffee?'

Rita shook her head. 'No, thanks. I won't stop. I just come to see how you were.' She sank down on to a chair. 'I still can't believe it happened. Muriel must have been mad.'

'Yes.' Thea agreed with a shrug as she sat down opposite. 'What I still can't work out is how she knew

I was getting married to Matthew. We told no one.'

Rita coloured alarmingly, and Thea looked at her in surprise.

'You didn't tell her? You couldn't have. I didn't tell you.'

'No, you didn't. And that's what got right up my nose.' Rita lowered her head. 'I saw you in town last Saturday, when you were shopping. I called to you, but you either didn't see me or chose to ignore me. I went after you to give you a bit of my mind, but lost you in the store. I saw you again in the wedding department where you were ordering your dress, and I heard you telling the salesgirl to book it to Matthew's account.'

Thea shook her head. 'I didn't see you.'

'I know.' Rita snorted. 'You walked straight by me on the way out. As close to me as you are now. And I was so stunned, I just let you go. Oh, God!' She groaned and put her head into her hands. 'If it wasn't for my vile temper, perhaps none of this would have happened.'

'Rita, what do you mean?' Thea's heart was beginning to thud. 'You weren't involved, were you?'

Rita shook her head. 'Only indirectly. I was so annoyed with you for not confiding in me that when I bumped into Muriel later I told her what I'd seen and heard, and ranted on a bit about the kind of friend you turned out to be. I probably tipped the balance in her crazy mind.' She looked up, her face white and shaken. 'Oh, Thea! Do you think I did?'

'I don't know.' Thea reached across and patted her knee reassuringly. 'But I'm sure she already had something bad lined up for me. Those files that kept going missing—I'm certain in my own mind that it was Muriel who was taking them. Perhaps she thought that if I had the sack for inefficiency, Matthew would take her back.' She shrugged. 'She thought she was in love with him. Who knows what was going on in her mind?'

Rita grasped Thea's hand. 'If you'd burned in that fire, I'd never have forgiven myself.'

Thea shook her head. 'But I didn't. And Muriel will probably get off with probation or something, so I think the best thing we can do is try to forget about it.'

Rita stood up. 'It will be a long time before I'll be able to do that. And from now on, I'll keep my big mouth shut.'

Thea smiled. 'Until the next time you're in a temper.'

Rita grinned sheepishly. 'You're probably right.'

'Matthew I'm stuck. Can you help?'

Matthew came out of the bathroom in his robe. 'In trouble?' He eyed her laconically.

Thea narrowed her eyes at him. 'If you say "again" I'll hit you.'

Matthew grinned and wrapped his arms about her. 'Our first fight already. And the honeymoon hasn't even begun.'

Thea snuggled closer into his embrace. 'And it's never going to unless you can get this damned zip undone.'

He laughed, his breath warm and tantalising against her ear. 'There's more than one way to cook a goose.'

Thea pulled back to look indignantly into his laughing eyes. 'A cooked goose is hardly a romantic analogy for a bride.'

'No. But it's nourishing. If you were a goose, I'd eat you.' He took a playful bite from her neck. 'Mmm. delicious! Next course, please.'

A shiver of anticipation tingled up Thea's spine. It was so long since he'd held her like this, their lovemaking would be like a first, new experience. Was that why he'd chosen to keep her at arm's length until the wedding? To her, it had been torture. Now she knew it would be worth the wait.

He turned her around to face away from him and the zip glided effortlessly downwards. He brushed the dress from her shoulders and let it fall at her feet. His arms slid around her from behind and, bending his head, he buried his lips in the sensitive hollow where her shoulder met her throat.

'Nothing wrong with that zip,' he murmured against her skin. 'Are you sure you weren't just trying to tempt me?'

Thea laughed. 'Would I waste my time?'

He turned her around again to face him and drew her close.

'That's the wonderful thing about honeymoons. There's all the time in the world.' He kissed the corner of her mouth, her eyelids and then the other corner of her mouth. 'And I'm going to make the most of every minute.'

Thea knew a moment of panic.

'It was a wonderful wedding, wasn't it? Are you sure your mother likes me?'

He kissed her nose. 'She adores you. Just as I said she would.'

'Poor Aunt Edith couldn't stop crying. And Melissa looked positively beautiful.'

He covered her mouth briefly with his. 'Shut up, Thea.'

His hand slid up and slipped the catch of her bra. Thea gasped as he pulled the flimsy garment away and proceeded to remove her slip and pants.

'But Matthew,' she protested, 'I'm on my way to my bath.'

'I know. I've just been running the water for you.' He shrugged out of his robe. 'And I fully intend to join you. From now on we're going to be inseparable.'

Matthew kissed Thea deeply and satisfyingly, and the

electric touch of his naked body against her own sent currents of delight running through her. With his lips still covering hers, he lifted her up into his arms and carried her through into the bathroom.

THREE UNBEATABLE NOVELS FROM
W●RLDWIDE

STOLEN MOMENTS by Janice Kaiser   £2.75

To escape her tragic marriage Lacey Parlett kidnaps her daughter
and is forced into hiding. Now, with the FBI closing in, she is desperate
to stay anonymous – but one man is dangerously near to discovering
her secret.

SARAH by Maura Seger   £2.95

The first of three novels in top author Maura Seger's captivating saga
on the Calvert family introduces Sarah – a formidable woman torn
between the man she loves and a society she hates during the American
Civil War.

STRONGER BY FAR by Sandra James   £2.50

Kate McAllister's ex-husband has been kidnapped. With less than 48
hours to meet the ransom demands, she has only one option left. . .
one she had sworn never to take!.

**These three new titles will be out in bookshops from
April 1989.**

*Available from Boots, Martins, John Menzies, W.H. Smith, Woolworths
and other paperback stockists.*

Mills & Boon
WINTER
COMPETITION

How would you like a
year's supply of Mills & Boon Romances ABSOLUTELY FREE?
Well, you can win them! All you have to do is complete the word
puzzle below and send it into us by <u>30th June 1989.</u>
The first five correct entries picked out of the bag after that date
will each win a year's supply of Mills & Boon Romances (Ten
books every month - **worth over £100!**) What could be easier?

C	W	A	E	T	A	N	R	E	B	I	H
H	R	I	C	E	R	W	O	L	G	M	Y
I	F	R	O	S	T	A	O	E	L	U	Y
L	N	I	B	O	R	U	D	R	I	V	Y
L	B	L	E	A	K	B	W	I	I	N	F
T	O	G	L	O	V	E	S	E	A	R	R
S	O	S	G	O	L	R	W	I	E	T	E
T	T	C	H	F	I	R	E	L	R	O	E
S	K	A	T	E	M	Y	C	I	K	S	Z
I	Y	R	R	E	M	I	P	I	N	E	E
N	A	F	D	E	C	E	M	B	E	R	N
N	C	E	M	I	S	T	L	E	T	O	E

Ivy	Radiate	December	Star	Merry
Frost	Chill	Skate	Ski	Pine
Bleak	Glow	Mistletoe	Inn	
Boot	Ice	Fire		
Robin	Hibernate	Log		
Yule	Icicle	Scarf		
Freeze	Gloves	Berry		

**PLEASE TURN
OVER FOR
DETAILS
ON HOW
TO ENTER**

How to enter

All the words listed overleaf, below the word puzzle, are hidden in the grid. You can find them by reading the letters forwards, backwards, up or down, or diagonally. When you find a word, circle it, or put a line through it. After you have found all the words the remaining letters (which you can read from left to right, from the top of the puzzle through to the bottom) will spell a secret message.

Don't forget to fill in your name and address in the space provided and pop this page in an envelope (you don't need a stamp) and post it today. Hurry - competition ends 30th June 1989

Only one entry per household please.

Mills & Boon Competition,
FREEPOST,
P.O. Box 236,
Croydon,
Surrey CR9 9EL.

Secret message _____

_____

Name_____

Address_____

_____

_____

_____ Postcode _____

COMP5